COMMANDO

THE ROYAL MARINE SPACE COMMANDOS
BOOK 1

JAMES EVANS
JON EVANS

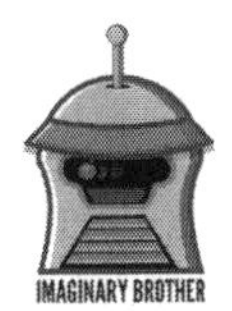

Cover art by Christian Kallias

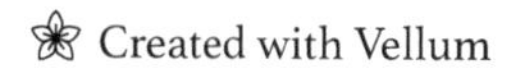

PROLOGUE

His heart pounded as he dodged and weaved, showers of earth and brick exploding around him. Ducking behind a solar array, he collapsed to the ground, gasping for air. He wrenched the rebreather from his face. A shard of plastic had buried itself in the filters; the thing was useless.

Angus could breathe the air, but it would be decades before the atmosphere was balanced. Without the oxygen from his mask, he couldn't run for long. Or run far.

He turned his head, risking a glance around the panel. Nothing. But they were there, somewhere, getting closer with every second that he lay still. He scrabbled around, hugging the ground while he got on his front and faced himself east, away from the panel and his would-be killers. He felt like a sprinter trying to get into the blocks, and that's what he needed to be.

There was an algal atmosphere recycler ahead of him and a moisture collector twenty metres to the north of it. The recycler was closer, but while it looked substantial, it was mostly plastic tubing and sheets, filled with a pale green mixture of algae and water. It was superb for increasing the atmospheric oxygen level but made for flimsy cover.

The moisture collector was a collection of turbines, metal fan blades, concrete posts and solar cells. Not sturdy as such but still a damned sight more bullet resistant than the recycler.

He made his choice and dashed forward, determined to take cover before he had to go to ground and let his heart slow down. The solar panel exploded as bullets ripped through it, scattering shrapnel that destroyed the nearby panels and drove dust high into the air.

Jones dove to his belly behind the concrete base of the moisture farm as more rounds sheared through the turbine above him with metallic screeches. At least he was on his front for the next sprint, and the concrete behind him felt like a much better shield. He lay there, sucking down the thin air while his heart rate slowed, looking desperately for his next dash.

Then he spied it, a pallet sled, left out here instead of returned to its dock at the homestead. For once that forgetful bastard Eric had done something useful, if only by accident. Jones looked wildly around. His ears were ringing from the gunfire, but he couldn't hear his pursuers. Whoever they were, he had to move. They'd be here soon; there was no time to spare.

He crawled towards the sled, shuffling over the dusty ground as quickly as he could. The sled was low to the ground, powered by solar cells built into its flat surface and designed to haul equipment around the compound. Unlike his lungs, it didn't run on oxygen. It might not be fast, but it was convenient, all-terrain and available.

He heaved himself onto it, pulled the control stick from the side and pressed the button. It moved slowly at first and then began to pick up speed once its sensors confirmed the load was stable. These things could match the pace of a hab vehicle, if need be, but they'd slow to a crawl if there was a risk that their load might fall off.

The speed began to mount, and Jones clung to the cargo straps, keeping flat, cheek pressed to the sled's base. With his newfound speed, the main buildings of their hab were soon in sight. Eric must've been in the workshop, but Gillian was outside, tending to the greenhouses. Gillian looked up as Jones began to shout, jaw dropping when she saw him on his unusual transport.

No! Not towards me, he thought. *Run to the vehicles, we have to get out of here!*

He shouted, as loud as he could, "Run! Get out of here! They're coming!" but his friend couldn't hear or didn't understand.

He rammed the control down to the highest setting and the sled sped up again, hurtling across the open ground. She still couldn't hear his terrified warnings, so he got up on one knee and screamed.

The sled bounced over a bump, just a small one, but he was thrown clear, tumbling and spinning through the dust. His arms flailed uselessly until he came to a sudden stop against a mound of fertiliser. His chest heaved as he fought for breath and he winced at the sudden pain in his chest. *A broken rib, maybe two*, he thought as pain lanced through him.

A hundred metres to go, he staggered to his feet, running now in a low crouch with one arm wrapped around his chest. His eyes watered, his chest burned with the effort, his ribs stabbed at him. He waved his free arm and cried weakly, "Run, Gillian!"

She stopped, staring, eyes wide in confusion.

"Aliens, Gillian, for fuck's sake, run! Invasion," he croaked as she finally got close enough to hear.

She had known Angus Jones for years and he had always been solid, reliable and dull. Now he was half out of his mind, raving about an alien invasion? Across all the solar systems mankind had settled, they had never encountered intelligent alien life. Perhaps he was suffering from oxygen deprivation; he had dropped his rebreather. Was he dangerous?

These thoughts and more ran through her head at lightning speed as Jones drew near, staggering along in obvious pain. Then Angus's skull vanished in a spray of red mist and his body collapsed in the dust.

There was a loud crack, and her face and overalls were suddenly covered with a fine wet coating. She looked down at the blood and fragments of bone on her chest and began to scream, unable to understand what was happening.

A distant voice called out to her, asking her what was wrong. Eric never got an answer. As he came out of the workshop, wiping his hands on a cloth, he saw Gillian standing there, screaming her head off. Then her head was gone and Eric screamed too.

"Get the wormhole channel open, now!" Governor Denmead shouted as she crouched behind the concrete wall of the balcony, looking down the sight of her rifle and scanning for the enemy. The sound of fully automatic gunfire could be heard in the distance. That had to be the enemy. The sporadic single shots were the colonists, fighting for their lives with light rifles, mining lasers and sheer bloody-mindedness.

"Governor," her aide, Johnson, shouted from the office, "we're through!"

Denmead saw movement, a bulky figure aiming a large weapon around a habitat in the distance.

"Be right with you," she murmured. She squeezed the trigger slowly as she steadied her breath and aimed. There was a crack and the rifle bucked in her hand. It was a good shot: the enemy took the round in the neck rather than right between the eyes, but he fell back out of view all the same. These low calibre semi-automatic rifles were issued to all new colonies to keep any local wildlife at bay or deal with the rare instances of banditry or maybe even occasional unrest. They weren't intended for armoured opponents wielding good-quality military gear. For that, they needed the Royal Marines.

She scrambled back into the office and slid behind the desk with Johnson. It wasn't dignified, but then neither was finding out the hard way that an enemy sniper had found a perch with a view through the windows of City Hall.

"This is Governor Denmead. Who am I speaking to?"

"Sergeant Wainwright, Governor. Please verify your ID and explain the situation," the man on the screen said calmly.

"We're under attack," Denmead began as she put her palm on the scanner.

"ID authenticated, Governor. What kind of attack? Civilian, pirates, corporate?" the sergeant asked, cool as a cucumber.

"I don't fucking know," she yelled, her self-control slipping momentarily as staccato series of bangs made the desk judder. "They started attacking outlying areas of New Bristol several days ago, and we didn't hear immediately because they killed everyone at those sites. Now they're attacking Ashton, and we're losing a lot of people. They have armour and military grade weaponry. That's as close as we've got to identifying them," she said.

"Do you require assistance from 42 Commando, ma'am?" the sergeant asked.

She almost lost her rag at that point. "Yes, we require some fucking assistance! You need to activate the Marines immediately and get the fleet on its way!"

"How many enemy combatants are there, ma'am?" Wainwright asked.

Gunfire erupted from outside, and a few rounds bounced off the walls of the building. The enemy was getting closer.

"We don't know. We've killed a few but more keep coming. They're pushing us back all the time. Did you hear that gunfire?"

"Yes, ma'am."

"They're just outside my office. We need to move before this area is overrun," Denmead yelled over the noise outside.

"Very well, Ma'am. Get yourself somewhere safe. I've requested the activation of the Marine clones in New Bristol. Please re-establish contact with us as soon as you are secure. Your request for Naval deployment has been noted. If we can get more detail, it would help make your case, Governor. The Navy is only deployed if a major threat is confirmed. Good luck, Governor. 42 Commando HQ, signing off," Wainwright said before cutting the signal.

"Help make our case?" she groaned as her eyes met Johnson's. He looked panicked. She probably did too. At least they would soon have help from military-grade clones, the Royal Marine Space Commandos that were issued to every new colony. They would help the colonists of New Bristol fight back. She just wasn't sure it would be enough.

1

Atticus snapped awake, the first breath tasting like fresh mountain air in his new lungs. For a moment, all was calm and peaceful. Then a dull crump rattled the building and brought dust from the ceiling. Time to go to work.

As he rolled to his feet, he was already reviewing the briefing installed while the pod had been bringing him round. An attack, assailant unknown, on a New British Empire colony planet.

Atticus checked his clock chip; twenty-four minutes had elapsed between Governor Denmead's call for help and his company being injected via wormhole. It had taken a further six hours to decant their bodies. Almost a record turnaround. Whatever this was, it was being taken seriously.

He dressed quickly as around him the rest of the command team, all wearing standard RMSC combat clones, and A Troop of Company 971, 42 Commando, pushed themselves from their pods. Secure lockers disgorged combat gear, and within minutes his team was fully equipped, ready to face whatever was waiting.

"Sound off," called Atticus, issuing the command audibly and as text into his combat HUD. His command team and A Troop called in with practised efficiency, their names appearing on the ID strips on their uniforms and in their HUDs.

Atticus nodded, content, as more explosions shook the building.

"Nothing from B Troop," said Colour Sergeant Stephanie Jenkins, "could be a comms problem." That was optimistic, and Jenkins knew it. The comms kit was ultra-reliable, battle-tested over more worlds than she could count. A Troop knew it as well and fell silent as they processed the implications.

"Assume nothing," murmured Atticus, checking his weapons one last time before giving the order to move out.

Weapons raised, A Troop climbed the stairs and fanned out into the corridors above the emergency deployment bay. Their HUDs showed a map of the compound with blinking blue dots for civilians and red for invaders, the information drawn from sensors all over the colony.

Worryingly large parts of the map were shaded grey where sensors had failed or lost contact.

"Captain, at last," came a new voice, tense with worry but flooded with relief. Atticus turned to find a stern woman hurrying towards him with a hunting rifle slung over her shoulder. She glanced across the assembled Marines, their builds so similar it would be difficult to tell them apart, despite the differing faces. "I'm Governor Denmead. Please, this way."

"Captain Atticus, Governor," he replied, shaking her hand, "and this is Lieutenant Warden. Can you update us? There were no details in the briefing," he asked.

"Good to meet you, despite the circumstances," she replied as they followed her along a corridor that led out of the building, "and all I can really tell you is that we're under attack from an unknown force."

"Governor, we can't reach the second EDB on comms. Do you have any idea of its status?" asked Atticus.

Governor Denmead shook her head. "I'm sorry, no. We've lost parts of Ashton's sensor grid and there are system failures elsewhere.

We don't have an up-to-date picture of the intact buildings. We're just trying to survive."

"Understood. Warden," said Atticus, "get to the second EDB, find B Troop, rendezvous when you can. Take Wilson in case there's a tech problem with the pods themselves."

"It's off to your west, or at least, that's where we built it, Lieutenant," the governor said as they emerged from the building into the thin air of New Bristol.

"Thank you, Governor. Sir," said Lieutenant Warden, "Section 1 with me." He led them away at a swift trot, following the directions in his HUD for the location of the second marine deployment facility.

Atticus and the rest of A Troop followed Denmead through the compound towards the fighting. As they ran, she gave a quick description of all that had happened.

At the edge of the building, they paused. Beyond, across a short stretch of open ground, stood City Hall.

"So fast, Captain, it was so fast," said the governor as she shrugged her weapon from her shoulder.

"How many of them, ma'am?" asked Atticus as he stared across the city, searching for the enemy.

"Scores at least, Captain, possibly hundreds. Our dead..." she trailed off. The bodies were piling up; their numbers tracked in Atticus's HUD as their signals went offline, one after the other.

"How are the attackers armed?"

"Automatic rifles and sharp-shooters. Some sort of grenade launcher, I think. I haven't seen railguns or lasers. We've been fighting them as best as we can, pulling the children back and just trying to hold them off, but we have," she paused, holding up her rifle, "limited options."

Atticus nodded, "Right, get to your command post and try to pull your people back. We'll be laying down heavy fire, and I don't want them getting caught in it. Hughes, go with the governor and make sure the comms are working properly."

"Sir!" Hughes barked in acknowledgement as he turned and followed the governor.

There was a burst of gunfire from somewhere beyond City Hall. Outside, firing towards the Hall, according to their HUDs. Atticus signalled his troops forward, leading them out onto the open ground and quickly across.

"Campbell take Section 2, inside, sweep the building, head for the front. Section 3, with me, we'll flank them around the east of the building."

Atticus watched the Marines of Section 2 heading out, their brand new mil-tech clones in tip-top condition, equipment gleaming, uniforms as yet untainted by the muck of a new world.

Then he headed for the corner of the building and the dusty parkland beyond it. Section 3 followed him as Section 2 triggered the door controls and disappeared into the building. Atticus paused briefly as Section 3 flowed smoothly around the edge of the building, seeking the enemy. He watched their indicators, and those of Section 2, moving steadily across the map in his HUD.

Then he hefted his rifle and followed his troops, Sergeant Jenkins and Marine Butler at his side.

2

Atticus crouched behind a chest high concrete wall atop a squat building that housed what Governor Denmead assured him were dangerous, but not explosive, chemicals. Terraforming required sweeping, long-term changes to the atmosphere and soil of a planet. In the short term, what the colonists needed was massive hydroponic systems packed with the best nutrients chemistry could refine.

There were dozens of buildings like this across the city, all storing different resources that had been shipped in by unmanned supply craft before colonists arrived or else were being manufactured locally by the automated extraction plants the colonists had installed.

Powered armour and surveillance drones had changed the face of the battlefield but having a high vantage point from which to observe the enemy was still helpful. Atticus especially liked having two feet of brutally ugly concrete wall between him and the enemy. The building might be austerely functional, but the colonists had covered the roof with green matting, sunbeds and chairs. Not that there was much weather to enjoy, he supposed, but it was no worse than the average British seaside town.

He turned back to face Governor Denmead, wishing she hadn't

joined him but impressed that she was putting herself on the front line.

"What can you tell me, Governor? Anything about their weapons and equipment?"

"Some of them have powered armour but not all of them," she said.

Atticus took that news with aplomb. "You're certain?"

"Captain Atticus, I shot one in the face earlier today, and it barely fazed him. And I'm not the only one who's seen them in suits," she admonished him.

"Fair enough. It's unusual for brigands to have powered armour, but I'm sure we can take care of it," he replied.

"They have military clones as well," she went on as Atticus raised an eyebrow. Obtaining military-grade clones was not only utterly illegal for non-government bodies but also extremely difficult. The modifications built into such clones were strictly for combat use and even the Sol governments rarely deployed troops in such clones. Outside of a troop deployment ship, military-grade cloning bays were almost unheard of.

"What kind of modifications have you seen? Could they be fringe planet black market clones?" he said, suggesting these were inexpert hacks that the brigands might have jury-rigged onto civilian clones.

"Captain," said Denmead in a tone pitched to close the argument, "I've been around long enough to recognise a back-alley clone. This force has full-size wings for their scouts. Eight-foot-tall, heavy weapons grunts and reports of some kind of close combat trooper that was fully mutated with natural armour, bladed arms and fangs. They are definitely high-quality military clones," she insisted.

"Fangs?" asked Atticus sceptically.

Denmead shrugged. "That report might be a bit far-fetched," she admitted.

"Any idea where they're operating from?"

Denmead pulled a data slate from her jacket and projected an image on the concrete wall, a map of the central colonised areas of New Bristol.

"No, not yet," she said, tapping the slate and pinging a series of locations within thirty kilometres of Ashton, "I haven't had much time, but these are the places I think are most likely. I've made a lot of assumptions, of course, and I'm not a military expert. Everyone in the outlying settlements is dead or here with us in Ashton, in fact. They could be using any of the outlying sites."

"How long have they been here?"

"We don't know," Denmead said, flinching as a burst of fire echoed from a nearby street, "they attacked the most distant locations first. Atmospheric processors, automated mineral extractors, energy farms. Most elements of our terraforming infrastructure are distributed in small pockets in case of unexpected atmospheric conditions or accidents. Only larger sites that require regular attention have a team that live onsite; any others are visited on rotation. They'd probably been attacking us for days before anyone managed to survive long enough to raise the alarm."

"Do you have any working fab units capable of making small arms?"

"Yes, but nothing large scale," Denmead said.

"We'll take whatever you can produce. I'll authorise you to set them making military weapons," Atticus said. Through his HUD he sent a clearance code to the governor that would unlock the restricted military patterns held by the colony's fabricators, along with a priority list of items to manufacture.

"Thank you, Captain. Our weapons aren't much use against these clones or their powered armour."

"Can you show me where your teams are?"

Denmead tapped her slate again, and the projection on the wall showed a series of blue, green and red dots. Blue for citizens who had joined the improvised militia and green for non-combatants, who were mostly hiding in buildings back from the front line.

Great areas of red hatching showed ground already lost or where the enemy troops were known to be. She sent a data stream to Atticus and he reviewed it on his HUD. It was basic information, but the tactical overlay could absorb the feed and update the

Marines' maps once the drones started providing more accurate data.

With the data came the colonists' health statuses, streamed from their personal monitoring bracelets. It was less comprehensive than the information Atticus had on his Marines but just knowing where people were and whether they were injured or dead was invaluable.

"It's time to pull your people back, Governor. We'll take over and we don't want your people getting caught in the crossfire," Atticus.

"I understand. Where do you want our line? My people have children to protect."

"Here, here and there, are good." Atticus pointed at a few buildings that would give good sight lines around the colony and allow the militia to act as a rearguard for his teams.

"Very well, I'll issue the order to fall back and then I'll retreat to our administrative backup here," Denmead said, indicating a reserve building which also held a cluster of green dots. "It's nothing special but it's got reserve power and access to most systems in case of a major problem with city hall."

"Roger that, Governor. Best of British to you," Atticus said as she made her way back down from the roof.

3

"Coming up on EDB two in one hundred metres, sir," said Corporal Goodwin.

"A lot of smoke here. Something's wrong. Fan out, keep to cover. Goodwin, get a drone up," ordered Lieutenant Warden. It wasn't necessary to order his Marines to take cover, they all had more experience than he did, but it needed to be a habit. Someday, he would have brand new marines to look after and they would need his guidance.

Goodwin had already thrown a micro-drone, shaped like a giant dart, in as high an arc as she could. It unfurled and stabilised as its rotors activated. An icon appeared in Warden's heads-up display to indicate there was a recon drone actively broadcasting video.

<Section 1, advance by numbers> Warden ordered sub-vocally, the words appearing in text on each Marine's HUD to ensure commands were received, regardless of the volume or background noise.

"Got anything, Goodwin?" asked Sergeant Milton, not taking her eye from the sight of her carbine as she scanned the buildings ahead.

"Not yet, Sarge. Want me to have a shufty?" Goodwin asked.

"Get your bird out there, Goodwin. I want to know where that smoke is coming from before we get there," Warden said.

The tiny drone, not much larger than the hummingbird it imitated, darted forward scanning the combat zone ahead. Goodwin would be concentrating on the video feed, the infra-red and sonar information that the drone provided. Milton was tailing her close, much like a spotter looking after her sniper. If anything happened, Milton would have Goodwin down and in cover even if she was distracted by the wealth of data she was monitoring.

They'd made two advances, one group dashing to the next available cover while another covered them, then sprinted to safety themselves, before Goodwin received an update.

The icon blinked in Warden's view and Goodwin's message scrolled across his HUD.

<Bay B destroyed>

Warden swore under his breath. He ducked behind a concrete waste bin as the drone's feed expanded into his HUD.

The cloning bay, technically an RMSC Emergency Deployment Bay, was a squat concrete building with a staircase running up the outside and a high-bandwidth comms array on the roof. Or at least, it had been. Now, it was little more than rubble. The bay, effectively a bunker, had lost its north wall and its roof had collapsed.

Normally the bays were buried, hidden from hostile eyes beneath tons of soil or concrete, but build details were determined by the colonists and the local conditions. Colonies had considerable operating leeway and could make their own decisions about building deployments. It was part of the attraction of life on a frontier world.

In Ashton, the second bay had been built in the open. The bay that Atticus and A Troop had decanted into was underground in the basement of a solar plant control room, much better protected.

Goodwin sent the drone through the hole in the north wall, checking the damage. The message <Breaching charge> flashed across Warden's HUD. He didn't ask how she knew; Goodwin was a highly trained tech specialist and if she said it was a breaching charge, it was a breaching charge. *So,* he thought, *the wall had been an entry point to the bunker?*

They had targeted the cloning facility, presumably to destroy it and cripple the RMSC's response capability. That suggested a level of tactical thinking that was unusual in a bandit attack. Whoever the enemy was, they were far too aggressive, too well equipped and too skilled to be treated lightly.

He sent a direct query back to Goodwin, <Recent? Still here? >, then issued a command to hold position to the rest of the section. They all hunkered down, eyes scanning the surrounding buildings, searching for signs of the enemy.

<No more than an hour> she replied.

The enemy was likely still nearby.

The drone darted straight up, and Warden flinched at the sudden shift. Techs did this all the time, but he found it disorienting. *There's a reason I didn't go into an Intel Group*, he admitted to himself.

With a wide view of the area, Goodwin was able to switch to a search mode, focusing on movement, heat profiles, radiation, comms traffic and any other sign of the enemy's location.

A sea of data and strange imagery swam in front of Warden's eyes for a few seconds before the chaotic colours and dozens of icons went back to the live feed again. This time, a building to the east of the bay was highlighted, a tall, thin structure, five storeys high, with large panes of glass held in place by a web of foamcrete. Cheap, lightweight and easily constructed, it was unquestionably office space.

All heads in the section swivelled towards it, and the Marines began to reposition themselves without his having to give an order.

Goodwin and Milton caught up with him, using the building on the corner of the crossroads as cover until they could join Warden behind his waste bin on the pavement. "Numbers?" he asked quietly. The lance-corporal shook her head; she didn't know.

He pondered their options. This felt like a raiding group. They could hear gunfire in the distance, but these troops were here to target valuable assets. If they were a military force from another colonial government, they'd be highly trained specialists, just like his Marines. He was confident of his team's abilities, but nobody was immune to a sniper round, and they didn't have any heavy weaponry, let alone powered armour. It wasn't part of the emergency deployment package for a colony this size.

B Troop wasn't going to be joining them anytime soon. It would take days to grow more clones, even if they could hold the remaining bay. The civilian bay would be a poor alternative, producing less advanced bodies in smaller numbers.

If he charged in without more information, he could very well lose all his Marines. On the other hand, if they sent the drone in, they might reveal themselves to an otherwise oblivious enemy and lose the advantage of surprise.

What was the enemy's plan? The team that had taken down the bunker had been quick, discreet and efficient. Warden's Section was probably being watched, but they hadn't been engaged, so maybe the enemy had targets and orders to avoid conflict. If that were the case, they'd be going for something else of high value, probably the remaining cloning bay or a power facility. Every building contributed to the energy grid but taking out a sizeable generation plant would impact their production of clones and equipment.

Warden shook his head. The decision was easy.

"Goodwin, get me a view inside. I want numbers, locations and armament." He signalled everyone else to be ready to lay down heavy fire. It wouldn't be subtle, but if Goodwin could get locations, they could tear through that building even with their basic carbines.

The drone dived, swooping towards a balcony on the top floor. It settled on a narrow upper pane and began to cut through the glass with its laser. It was inside the building in seconds, flitting through the offices and confirming the floor was empty in under a minute. It did an abrupt flip that made Warden's stomach lurch and rolled to the atrium that plunged through the building.

Righting itself, it zipped into the offices on the fourth floor, angling for the corner that faced Warden's position. Six figures lit up ahead, and their locations popped on the HUDs of the Marines. Warden saw a glimpse of powered armour before one of the figures turned and raised a small hand weapon. There was a flash, and the feed went black. His HUD automatically went back to the default view; the drone's icon gained a red cross to show it was disabled.

"Son of a bitch!" Goodwin cried out. "Lieutenant, permission to engage?"

"Granted, Lance-Corporal," he said, turning to face the building in a crouch and bringing his carbine to bear. The icons on his HUD showed the last known location of each enemy.

Goodwin answered the destruction of her equipment with a two-pronged approach. First, the defunct drone detonated with an almighty noise and a light bright enough to blind. Secondly, she brought her carbine to bear and with a triple popping noise and a panning motion, expertly fired three grenades through windows on the fourth, third and second floors, one above the other.

The detonations were nigh on simultaneous, a staccato cacophony that could be felt as a bass rumble in their chest. It was accompanied by bursts of fire from the entire section. Goodwin had already thrown another drone and Warden could hear her cursing the enemy under her breath and vowing revenge.

It came quickly. As the clouds of dust billowed out and the drone's data reached their HUDs, the Marines could see the softly glowing outlines of four figures on the ground floor. Two more were outlined in blue, lying prone in the rubble.

As soon as the drone pinged the enemy powered armour units, Warden's section opened fire. Each marine fired bursts with expert precision into the dust cloud, guided by the drone's sensors. They were rewarded with the distinctive metallic pings of bullets striking powered armour.

"Grenades!" ordered Warden and a flurry of ordnance arced across the open space, detonating directly on or near the blue outlines as the drone skipped back to avoid the blasts.

The final grenade detonated at the roof of the building, still hanging precariously above the vacant space below it. It collapsed with a resounding crash, directly on top of the enemy position.

Warden glanced to his left and saw a smug grin on Milton's face. He nodded in approval and turned to Goodwin.

"Survivors?" he asked.

She jabbed at her drone interface a few times and shook her head. "Can't say for certain, sir, but no signs of life."

"Take a breather, folks. Let's see if any of those bastards get up," Warden cast over the comms.

"No movement, no energy signatures, sir," Goodwin announced a minute later.

"Let's move in then," Warden said as he ordered the advance via the section's HUDs.

They moved across the open ground, weapons trained on the pile of rubble that was all that remained of the corner of the building. The explosions had strewn debris all over the street, leaving everything within fifty metres of the shattered structure covered in dust and grime.

Goodwin's drone shot straight up, climbing to two hundred metres before it began to follow a spiral holding pattern, scanning a much broader area for signs of life, enemy or ally.

Warden pulled a pocket open on the neck of his jacket and slid an air filter up from it to cover his mouth and nose. It wasn't capable of protecting him from an active weapons attack, but it was ideal for sandstorms or billowing clouds of concrete dust and particulates. Most of the section followed suit; their HUDs already protected their eyes.

Something clanked against his boot, and he looked down at a prone armoured trooper lying in the dust. He stepped back and brought his weapon to bear. Milton moved up beside him and reached down to pull back a sheet of wall fibre, which covered the apparent corpse. No response.

"Do you recognise this armour pattern, Sergeant?"

"No, sir, never seen anything like it. It's thin. Delicate," she said as she knelt beside the corpse and rolled it over. The chest was buckled in, probably from the direct force of one of the grenades. Still, Warden would have expected it to have torn the trooper limb from limb if it had hit directly. Even powered armour wasn't invulnerable to a close-range detonation.

The head was crumpled too, not quite flat but damaged enough to give the owner a fatal headache. There were no markings on the suit that he recognised, in fact, no markings at all. It was a dull grey with a strangely shimmering surface.

Milton grabbed it by the joint at the neck and hauled the body upright. She turned to him with a puzzled look. "It's light. I mean, really light, sir. Russian-made, maybe? Or American?"

Warden nodded towards it. "Look at that." The suit had changed colour as she lifted it from the dust-covered rubble. "Some sort of chameleon coating."

"That's a new one on me. I'd keep it quiet if I'd developed that too. No wonder they got so far into the city without anyone noticing. I bet we wouldn't have even found them without the drone," Milton said.

"Ultra-light power armour designed for stealth by an unknown power," he mused, shaking his head. "No way bandits get hold of gear like this. Could be an actual covert action by a Sol government."

"I bloody well hope not, sir. Why would anyone even want this rock? It's not even halfway terraformed yet. It'll be, what, twenty or thirty years before this shit-hole starts to look habitable to normal people," she said.

"Maybe there are resources on New Bristol our teams didn't find. What's the alternative? That some underworld group managed to build an entirely new type of power armour? Maybe they attacked a top-secret lab that some government put on a remote asteroid base?" Warden scoffed.

"Yeah, well, I didn't say I had a better explanation, I just don't see any Sol government sending a strike force here. It's a huge risk for not very much reward. Well over a century since the last intra-Sol war and this would risk another." Milton shrugged.

Warden nodded thoughtfully and sent a comm request to Captain Atticus.

"Lieutenant?" came the terse response.

"Sir, Bravo Bay has been destroyed. We encountered an enemy

infiltration unit in some kind of light powered armour in a stealth configuration. They'd breached the bunker, set charges and looked to be heading towards Bay Alpha. We slotted them," Warden reported.

"One second," said Atticus, a burst of fire accompanying his response.

Warden turned to Goodwin.

"Get me a city-wide picture. The captain and Section 3 are bogged down in a firefight and we need to know where they are and what they're facing," he ordered while he waited for Atticus to come back to him.

"We're heavily engaged. Power armour here as well but nothing light about it. They have enhanced troops too," Atticus said as explosions went off in the background.

"They have military-grade clones?"

"Yes, and the powered armour to go with them. We have a serious problem here. We need a force multiplier, and that leaves only one option," Atticus said.

"Civilian clones?"

"Yes," Atticus said, patching in Governor Denmead. "Governor, our second bay has been destroyed. What shape are your bays in?"

"Shit. Let me check," Denmead replied. "No, we used most of our standby clones already and the facility has taken some damage. It's not able to accept downloads or start incubating new clones."

"Noted. Incubation would take a few days anyway. In that case, Warden, check what remains of Bay Bravo. If there are any military-grade weapons or material there, get them to Governor Denmead. Check the bodies, scavenge their weapons too, then double-time it to my position and get stuck in," Atticus ordered. "Signing off."

Warden took a deep breath and called his section, updating them face to face. Inefficient, maybe, but a better way of breaking the bad news. They took it surprisingly well, but they were Royal Marine Space Commandos and had the best part of a millennium of predecessors to live up to. Impossible odds were nothing to get all weepy over.

"Sir, you'd best take a look at this," said Milton.

"What's up?" He walked over to the sergeant, who was kneeling beside one of the power armoured corpses, and crouched beside her.

She leaned to one side so he could see what she was looking at. The helmet the soldier wore had been removed and his face was exposed. Or its face, rather. It wasn't human, not even vaguely. It wasn't just the eyes; the whole face was inhuman. Military clones sometimes had modified eyes, particularly snipers, but nothing like the black orbs that now stared, lifeless, at Milton.

Scales covered the face, the nose was flattened and shielded with a thick plate, rather like a lizard. The bone structure wasn't right either, too smooth, too ovoid, and the eyelids seemed reptilian. It was like looking at a humanoid dinosaur, something you'd see in a holo-show.

Warden looked at Milton, at her raised eyebrows and back down at the reptilian face.

"No," he said.

"Yes."

"No, absolutely not."

"Yes, Lieutenant."

"You want me to believe this is an alien, don't you?"

"No, I want it to be some kind of base layer balaclava they wear under their armour, but I already tried pulling it off. It's definitely got scales and it's definitely not human," said Milton.

"Well. Bollocks."

"Sounds about right. So, shall we get on with it, then?"

4

Warden's feet pounded the concrete as he ran towards Captain Atticus's current position. There'd been a heavy firefight up here and the colonists were hunkered down to the south. A HUD replay of their positions showed that Section 3 had pressed the enemy hard, forcing them back into an underground facility. He jumped over an enemy body and crouched behind the concrete base of a communications relay tower as he assessed the situation.

Around him, his section took a breather. They'd sprinted over and were now only a hundred metres from the captain's position. Regrouping in cover was the smart move.

The alien soldier wore a face-covering helmet and unpowered armour so light that it offered almost no protection, but it was the long, elegant, wings that made it notable. They stood out, as did the long-barrelled rifle nearby. A sniper's clone, with wings to help it to reach vantage points that would otherwise be inaccessible.

The replay showed the dots that represented Atticus and Section 3 descending into the underground hydroponic and storage facility to pursue the aliens. That was the way of the Commando; press the advantage, keep advancing, never give the enemy time to regroup.

They weren't about to worry about the presence of the first aliens humans had encountered. They knew their job, and they'd do that as efficiently as possible. Time to worry about aliens later; for now, they were just another enemy to defeat.

Goodwin's drone reported no enemy movement above ground. Reports were fuzzy from below ground where Atticus's team were, and Warden's HUD reported only a sixty-five per cent chance their location info was still correct. There should have been a network mesh in the facility, but either the colonists hadn't seen fit to install it or it had been damaged in the fighting. Either way, they would have to do this the old-fashioned way until they were underground and started to get reliable readouts from the Marines in Section 3. There was a gristly sound behind him and Warden turned to see Milton putting a blade into the neck of the sniper, just to be sure. Caution was sensible but there was no point wasting ammunition.

"Advance," he whispered, his voice carried clearly to each commando via their HUDs. They moved the last hundred metres, going from cover to cover, watching everything, scanning the skies. Where there was one winged alien sniper, there would doubtless be more, and the colonists had any number of relay towers, atmospheric processing units and even bio-engineered trees dotted around the city.

The entrance to the facility was still intact, though the greenhouse above it was nothing but a tangled mass of aluminium with a frosting of shattered glass. There was a goods elevator that all but screamed 'Obvious trap, die here'.

They took the wide concrete stairs, passing another alien corpse on the way. This one was in powered armour which had been pummelled with bullets; the entire section must have fired on it to do this much damage to powered armour with carbines. No need for Milton to draw her knife here.

The stairs led into a spacious garage for the electric carts used to ferry supplies around the colony. The elevator shaft was to their left, and Milton cautiously checked that it was empty as they advanced on the double doors in front of them. The garage was well lit but beyond the doors, the lighting seemed haphazard at best.

Warden tried the comms again but Atticus and his section were quiet, unanswering. Warden shook his head and pressed on.

Through the doorway was a large hydroponics hall, at least two storeys high and the size of a football field. It should have been flooded with light for the plants but even before they pushed the doors open, they could tell that the lighting was buggered.

There had been a gunfight. Smoke still hung in the air, and everywhere they saw the tell-tale signs of grenade damage. The planters were four-metre-high shelves full of crops in compost. Some of the rows were intact, but most were shot through or had been blown apart. The cover was poor, the earth in the planters barely sufficient to slow a bullet, and there was simply too much space between them to hide anything larger than a drone. The HUD showed more rooms directly opposite the double doors and to the north.

If the aliens had stopped in the hydroponics room and made a stand, the commandos would have been just as exposed as the enemy, so they'd have fallen back as quickly as possible to the next room. Warden checked his HUD. The plans were updating now, the accuracy percentage climbing rapidly as they came into range of the first members of Section 3.

They moved through the room at double time and found their first friendly casualty, a body so badly damaged even the HUD couldn't tell who it had been. The death would have been recorded by his colleagues' HUDs, so there was no point in stopping to confirm. Milton ordered the Marines bringing up the rear to strip the weapons and ammunition from the deceased, and they did so with grim efficiency as the rest of Section 2 advanced.

There were two sets of double doors, all peppered with dents and bullet holes. Atticus and his Marines had fired on the fleeing enemy, chasing them into this pit. They must have been here scant minutes earlier, leaving behind only shell casings as they hunted the enemy troopers.

The doors were spaced several metres apart, but both opened into the same chamber. Marines gathered on either side of each pair of doors, ready to rush in once they were opened.

It was a warehouse, filled with large shelving units all stacked with pallets of boxes. The aisles were wide enough for forklifts, and more goods elevators waited against the east and west walls. The HUD showed a maze of rooms behind the north wall. Office space, judging by the size and layout. The dots indicating the surviving members of Atticus's team were clustered in that area.

"Shit," muttered Warden, looking at his team and trying to not to get distracted by the shadows.

Warden hit the open button next to him, and the doors slid quickly back into the walls, his Marines flowing through the opening as he double-timed it down the aisle. Visibility in here was better, at least in the aisle itself, and the overhead lamps still filled the room with a sickly white glow. There was no sign of gunfire in the warehouse. The Marines spread out, small groups going down each aisle to properly clear the room, carbines pointing at all corners and up towards the ceiling, looking for hidden enemies.

"Captain? Are you reading me?" Warden asked as he hastened down the aisle.

A message flashed in his HUD.

<Pinned down. Resistance heavy, casualties rising, ammunition low. Have a flesh wound. Can't speak, would compromise position>

<Understood. Stay in cover. We've almost reached you> Warden sent back.

Seconds later, they approached the far side of the warehouse and could see into the office space. The offices and other rooms were constructed with stud walls to break up another large room, probably the same size as the warehouse and hydroponic farm rooms. There were two floors of rooms, but no indicators showed any of the marines upstairs.

They didn't need their HUDs to see that the walls provided no cover. There were bullet holes, scorch marks and shattered windows everywhere.

Warden was reasonably sure if he fired at one of the walls there was a good chance his round would make it all the way to the other side of the huge space. *Shit,* he thought, *that wasn't helpful.*

Not having cover was one thing. Having the semblance of cover was worse. You couldn't see the enemy, and it was tempting to stop behind something that seemed solid. Once you did that, your enemy could just shoot through whatever you had ducked behind. Better to have an open space that didn't impede movement than this mess.

He could already see a few corpses, though there was so much dust and debris that he wouldn't have been sure they were marines if his HUD hadn't identified them. A burst of gunfire came from the alien's direction, and sure enough, the bullets shattered glass and punched through walls as if they were tissue paper, impacting in the concrete of the wall separating the offices from the warehouse.

"Milton, we're going to have to rush through here. No one stop for casualties; we need to force them back," he ordered.

Quickly they issued orders to the section. Warden would head for the captain, who was about twenty-five metres away through a series of walls and offices. Milton would go left with a small team, hoping to flank the enemy and make it to the northwest corner of the concrete chamber before pressing them. The rest would fan out to provide covering fire, using combined readouts from infra-red sights and their HUDs to force the aliens to keep their heads down.

"Go," Warden said, simultaneously issuing the command via the HUD as well. The entire group rushed through the various doors and set about their tasks. As soon as Milton's team had veered left and Warden had started his crouched sprint towards Captain Atticus, the covering fire began. Wilson followed him; the tech specialist looked grimly determined, clearly peeved that the captain had been injured. The Marines fired as they moved, expertly suppressing the enemy with short bursts from their carbines.

Goodwin's drone made an almost certainly suicidal dash down the corridors and through shattered window holes, trying to get close enough to the enemy positions to reveal them on the HUD. If they could get a good enough update, the marines could target the aliens directly, and Atticus's team would be able to join in. They were scattered throughout the southern half of the space, probably all lying prone to avoid getting shot by the aliens' seemingly indiscriminate fire.

Warden would have given anything for a clear arc of fire. A few grenades might have made the difference but down here, in this mess, it would be an unacceptable risk.

With all the shredded walls and bundles of cabling dangling from semi-collapsed ceilings, he could imagine a grenade bouncing back towards his position and devastating his section. Instead, he fired a burst from his carbine in the general direction of the doors and made another sprint towards the captain.

There was an answering burst of fire from the aliens, and though it missed him, it was close enough for him to dive through an open door and land unceremoniously on the carpet, skidding to a stinging halt.

"Fucking carpet burns," he murmured in disbelief as he bounced, lucky not to crack a rib. The cloned body might only be a loaner, but he needed it to do his job and, clone or not, a broken rib still stung like hell.

Injury indifference, they called it. It was a risk all cloned soldiers faced: the semi-suicidal use of a new body that wasn't, technically, their own. The Canadian Coalition forces had reported the same problem as their British allies. New soldiers took unnecessary risks for the first year or two until they realised just how painful the higher injury rate was and that nobody was going to grow them a new body simply because they broke an arm.

Warden gritted his teeth and scrambled forward, keeping low to the floor as his section continued to lay down covering fire. It wasn't particularly dignified crawling around on the floor of a cheaply furnished office, but it was ultimately going to be quicker and a lot less dangerous to reach the captain this way.

Plus it was easy enough to devote some brainpower to monitoring the HUD updates. Half of Atticus's section was already marked as terminal casualties. Colour Sergeant Jenkins and Marine Butler were dead. Not good, especially when they were facing enemies with powered armour and they didn't yet have the weapons or kit to counter that properly. They needed numbers to make up the difference.

A short dash down an easterly corridor and a sharp turn into an office brought him to a filing cabinet, not two metres from Captain Atticus, who was slumped by a similar cabinet further along the same wall.

"Lieutenant," the captain acknowledged through gritted teeth that glistened with blood.

"Sir. Bit of a sticky wicket?" Warden asked cheerfully, forcing a grin.

"I've had better days. You?"

"We meet some charming gentlemen, dressed for a nice afternoon stroll through a war zone, but they seemed much more agreeable after we dropped a building on them. Turns out they're not from these parts and don't have passports or identification."

Atticus coughed in wry amusement, then cursed and spat blood.

"So we discovered. They still don't like it up 'em. We met their colleagues, tenacious buggers. I can't say I ever thought this is what a First Contact situation would be like."

"Doesn't really fit the tactical assessment briefing we got on First Contact. 'No chance aliens would be hostile' they said. Million to one against, the Professor said."

"How does the old saying go? Million to one chances crop up nine times out of ten?"

"One of my favourite books, sir. How are you feeling?"

"Well. I don't mind telling you, Tom, that I don't feel too clever. I'm reasonably sure I'm not getting out of here."

"Hmm. I was hoping it was just a flesh wound," Warden replied as another cacophony of gunfire was exchanged above their heads.

"Fair to say that my flesh is definitely wounded," hissed Atticus.

"What are your orders, sir?"

"Can't hang around here, you have work to do. I'm passing command authority to you. Unless we get a cloning facility active, I won't be back for a while. Has Wilson made it?"

"So far, sir."

"Good, keep him safe, you'll need him. I've been coming up with a plan while I lie here trying to hold my guts in. The balance of probability," he said, pausing as a wave of pain passed through him, "is that these aliens use cloning technology, just like we do. Mostly humanoid but the wings and some other differences look like augmentations to me. None of the xenobiology theory I've seen suggests a species would develop to space-era technology and have such a wide variety of forms. Have a look at this," Atticus said, sliding an object across the floor to Warden.

He picked it up. It was a heavy calibre pistol, probably made for a power armoured hand. Nothing out of the ordinary.

"Notice anything strange?" Atticus asked, and when Warden shook his head, he suggested, "Pop the magazine out a moment."

Warden thumbed the release and caught the half-full magazine as it ejected from the grip of the weapon. The rounds looked like a fairly standard caseless design, probably 15mm which was large but easily handled by the servo-motors in powered armour. It seemed entirely normal. He shrugged and pushed the magazine home. "Not sure I get it, sir?"

"Just like a normal personal weapon that we'd issue to powered armour troopers as a backup, yes?"

Warden nodded, then frowned. Atticus could practically see the light dawning on his subordinate's face. *There it is, comprehension,* he thought. *At least the lad isn't entirely stupid.*

"Wait. Why is an alien weapon so similar to our own?"

"Exactly. You got that magazine out like you'd been using that weapon for years. Because you have. Every service pistol you've used has been pretty much the same as that design. How the hell did an alien species independently come up with the design we use, eh?"

"Well, they couldn't, that's just... Well. It's improbable, to say the least. They must have copied our designs from somewhere. That explains why their powered armour looks the way it does. All their kit, it's just their version of equipment from Sol. Where the hell did they get the designs, though?"

A burst of fire cut through the office, punching the cabinets and filling the air with paper.

"I've been thinking about that too," said Atticus as the Marines returned fire. "I think it was an Ark ship. I think that these aliens found one, could have been any of the missing ships or even one of the fleets. They captured it or found the ship derelict. Perhaps it even landed on their home planet." Atticus shook his head, aware he was rambling. "They ended up with all sorts of advanced engineering information and they were similar enough to us to make use of it. Now, they know we're out here somewhere, and they've planned an invasion."

"An invasion?" It sounded thin to Warden, but he had to admit the firefight certainly leant strength to Atticus's argument.

"This might not be the only alien attack underway at the moment. Regardless, you now know that they're using weapons and armour not that dissimilar to our own. That makes me think they're also using our cloning technology. We're not fighting real aliens, just their clones. They might not even be humanoid on their home planet. Maybe they used our form because it's more practical for this work? For all we know, they're avian or water dwelling. It doesn't matter. What does matter is that they probably get around the galaxy the same way we do because they're using our technology against us. They go somewhere in a ship on auto-pilot, download into clones and then drop out of orbit to begin their attack," Atticus said.

"Makes sense. The Lost Arks had a lot of the same technology we use now, and cloning is still the best way to get around the galaxy. All they lacked was faster than light drives. What's your plan then, sir? Not to be too pushy but our cover might not last long, and you're looking paler by the minute," Warden said apologetically.

"They must have a base of operations somewhere," Atticus screwed his eyes closed as another wave of pain wracked his body. "Gather the troops, get some transport and attack. Check the outlying stations. Start with the first to fall. They probably chose one with plenty of power and buildings, far enough from here to be secure and near enough to launch attacks. I haven't seen vehicles, so I think they're operating largely on foot. Speak to the governor, find their base, then capture or destroy their cloning facility to prevent them reinforcing. Questions?" Atticus said.

"After we've dealt with their base, we have to track any remaining enemy and destroy them," Warden agreed.

"Yes, then prepare the locals for any follow-up that might come and get any intelligence back to HQ. Other colonies in this sector may be at risk," Atticus said. "Try not to destroy their cloning bay, you might need it, and maybe Wilson can use some of the components to repair the colonist's bays, anyway," he advised.

"Right. Time to get you out of here then, sir," Warden said.

"Hah!" Atticus responded, coughing up blood as he tried to laugh off the suggestion, "I don't think that's a worthwhile use of resources. This body is done for. My HUD has four of them left in this squad, but the drone feed shows another squad on its way."

He paused, fingers grasping weakly for Warden's arm.

"You have about four minutes to get out of here. I'm staying right here where, if I'm very careful not to move too much, the pain won't get any worse. Leave any explosives you can spare, and as soon as their mates turn up, I'll throw a little welcome party." He paused again, then gave a tiny nod. "Now, get cracking. Three minutes and counting. You have your orders."

Warden stared at the captain for a second, then nodded with grim determination. He unslung a pack from his waist and withdrew a block of explosive and a detonator. As he did so, he issued orders over his HUD and Atticus announced the transfer of command. The commandos began a tactical withdrawal back the way they'd come, stopping by their fallen comrades to assist the injured and grab useful kit from those beyond help.

Warden moved quickly to Atticus's side and opened his med kit, withdrawing a pair of dispensers and slamming them into the captain's thigh. His eyes snapped open, suddenly alert from the booster and additional painkiller. Not medically advisable, given his condition, but it would keep him conscious long enough for him to enact his plan.

Then Warden removed the captain's explosive pack and slapped it together with his own. He grabbed a couple of flares from the captain's webbing and mashed them in as well, adding a detonator and syncing it to the captain's HUD.

Atticus grabbed his wrist, brow beaded with sweat. "Take my carbine. I can't hold it anyway. Give these bastards hell, Warden, you hear? When I come back, I want your report to say they're all dead and the citizens are safe."

"Yes, Captain," was all Warden could say as he laid a comforting hand on his shoulder and squeezed it.

They fell back into the warehouse as quickly as possible. The next message from Atticus read <Ninety seconds> and they began to run as fast as they could, abandoning covering fire as they dashed through the warehouse and into the hydroponic farm.

<Fifteen seconds. Atticus signing off until the next time> as they burst onto the staircase.

There was a distant chatter of gunfire, far away under the earth, then an almighty explosion ripped through the underground building. The captain's indicator on their HUDs went dead as a choking cloud of hot dust billowed up the stairs and into the thin atmosphere. More than a dozen icons, the alien troops and their reinforcements, winked out of existence at the same time. The captain had not sold his final moments lightly.

Warden looked around the remaining Marines, some coughing and spitting dust from their mouths, some looking angry, some depressed.

"No time for a brew, we have work to do. Get the drones up; I want to know if there's any enemy movement in the city. And find the governor. The captain had a plan and we're going to carry it out." He paused and looked around at his troops.

"We're taking the fight to the enemy."

5

Warden entered the conference room and leant on the back of a chair, head hanging as his chest heaved and his heart pounded in his chest. Under normal conditions, it wasn't far to run, but New Bristol's atmosphere didn't really encourage vigorous exercise. The air was breathable but you really noticed the lack of oxygen when you exerted yourself.

They had moved quickly once Captain Atticus had made his sacrifice. His plan required the support of the colonists and, if his supposition was correct, the aliens could be downloading into new clone bodies even now.

"Lieutenant, you don't look like a man bringing good news," Governor Denmead said, leaving the question hanging.

Warden engaged the safety on his carbine, withdrew the magazine and cleared the chamber. Then he put the weapon on the table and did the same with Captain Atticus's carbine and pistol. A set of webbing packs followed. He opened one, withdrawing an ammunition packet. Then he sat down and began to reload the captain's magazines. Once settled into the familiar rhythm, he looked up at the governor.

"I'm not, Governor Denmead. Captain Atticus is dead. He gave his life buying time for the rest of us to escape the hydroponic farm. He took a dozen aliens with him but we'd already lost good Marines before I arrived with Section 2," Warden reported.

The governor cursed in a most impolite manner before summoning her self-control.

"I'm sorry to hear that, Lieutenant. The captain was a good officer and he was surely a brave man. The citizens of New Bristol owe him a debt. I wish I had time to say more but I need to know what your plan is."

"You don't seem bothered by the idea that the attackers are aliens, Governor."

She levelled him a cold look. "I had already wondered about that, Lieutenant, but I wasn't going to be the first to say it. We've always known there must be intelligent life elsewhere in the galaxy and Sol governments have been preparing for it for hundreds of years. Don't you think I've taken the First Contact training courses? I've been sitting in xenobiology lectures and first contact briefings since before you were born. Most are about peaceful results, but there were enough scenarios like this that I'm not entirely shocked. If you say they're aliens, they're aliens. What matters is, can we hold them off, can we survive?"

"Glad to hear it, Governor, and yes, I think we have a chance."

Warden stood, picked up the captain's carbine and the two magazines he'd loaded and walked over to the governor. He placed them on the table in front of her. "I think you should have these now. You may need them soon and it's a serious weapon. You remember how to use one?" he asked.

"Yes, Lieutenant Warden. Basic training was some time ago but we get annual refreshers along with the keys to the colony and the launch codes for the orbital nuclear strike weapons." She paused then shook her head. "Sorry, too soon for jokes. There are always risks on remote colonies in the outer rim, but I wasn't expecting this," said Governor Denmead. Then for emphasis, she checked the weapon was safe, reloaded it and made it safe again. "Frontier Governor isn't a role for the fainthearted."

"Good. Before he died, Captain Atticus gave me orders to attack the aliens' base of operations. This is one of their pistols," he said, producing the large calibre weapon designed for powered armour wearing alien troopers. Demonstrating the mechanism, he went on, "As you can see, this is a human design. Updated and modified, certainly, but far too similar to be a coincidence. Atticus believed that the aliens encountered one of the Lost Arks and their equipment is based on designs found within it. That means it may be compatible with ours and they're likely using our cloning technology as well. With me so far? I don't have time to discuss this overly much, I'm afraid."

Governor Denmead nodded. "I'm with you, Lieutenant. I'll let you know if I have any questions which can't wait."

"They will have captured a location within easy reach of the city. If you've seen no sign of them using vehicles, then their base has to be within practical marching distance. A day of walking, maybe a little more, but no further than that. It must have good power supplies or a good range of buildings and be defensible. Anything else wouldn't have enough strategic value to be worth using. I need to know the likely candidates. After that, I need to know what vehicles you have that we can use to get there," Warden said.

Denmead put the carbine down and picked up her data slate. A wall screen flicked on, and a satellite imagery map of New Bristol appeared. She caught his look of surprise and answered the very question that was on his mind, "No, Lieutenant, our satellites are gone. This is last year's data. The topography and locations are correct, of course, but for all we know, the outposts depicted here," she zoomed the map out, "have been completely destroyed."

That was disappointing but not particularly surprising. An alien ship in orbit could easily have destroyed or disabled the colony's satellites. Surveillance by low-atmosphere drone was now their only option. Warden issued an order through his HUD, and the tech specialists shared their data with the governor's systems. The map of New Bristol began to update, showing the destroyed hydroponic farm and cloning bay.

"These are the largest outposts that might match your description," Denmead said as three locations on the map pinged. "All of these have some sturdy buildings, they're within a reasonable distance for troops to march on the city and they have decent energy supplies."

"May I?" Warden asked, holding his hand out for the slate. The governor nodded and passed it to him.

He worked the controls, viewing each site from various angles, examining the relief map. "I think we can rule these ones out, they're all on flat terrain. Cavendish Station has the right mix of buildings but it's overlooked by this outcrop here and far too easily attacked. I'd bet against Weston Farm as well; the ravine would make it difficult to get here quickly and efficiently."

"So that just leaves...North Solar Farm," Denmead said.

"What can you tell me about it?" Warden asked.

"Nothing interesting. There's a solar power plant there, obviously," she said pointing to an array of panels on the western side of the display. "There are some laboratory greenhouses there for testing plants that might survive outside a hydroponic farm. Then there's some accommodation and a storage bunker."

"Looks promising. What's this area here?" Warden asked.

"Land cleared for a new expansion. A concrete base prepped for new buildings."

"Must be a pretty big expansion, that has to be a hundred metres across. This is our best site. Landing a dropship there wouldn't be any problem at all; it's ideal. They know they've got a stable landing site, power, ready-made barracks and even a bunker. It couldn't be better for them if they'd sent you the specification themselves," Warden said.

"We have some rovers you can use to get out there. They're civilian vehicles, but they have good range and will cope with the terrain."

"Right, we need to get moving. We're going to leave you the spare weapons we recovered from our casualties. Have you managed to produce any of your own?" Warden asked.

"Not quite. The fabrication plants are still working on the materiel that Captain Atticus authorised. If you want to leave now, none of the weapons will be ready, but we should have plenty of ammunition. Do you want to wait?"

"No, we can't. We must press the advantage now. We'll restock at the armoury, release everything we don't need to you and then get stuck in. We captured a few enemy weapons and we'll test those en route, see if any will be of use. Beyond that, we're limited to the light, small arms the emergency bay armouries are equipped with. Grenades and a few sniper rifles are the heaviest we've got." Warden shrugged. "We'll make do."

"I wish I could help, Lieutenant, but we haven't the population or economy to justify rapid fabricators at this stage of the colony's development. They burn too much energy to be supported at the moment. If you came back in a few years," she said apologetically, letting the sentence die.

Warden grinned. "Governor, we're Commandos. Improvising our tactics and weapons is a regimental tradition."

6

The rovers made easy work of the rocky terrain between New Bristol and the unimaginatively named North Solar Farm. Not that that was surprising; their design had been refined and put to the test on dozens of colony worlds.

Most Sol governments used something similar and even the early Mars explorers would have recognised the basic design. Six large wheels, suitable for all terrain, computer controlled and with high-travel suspension.

Getting in quickly was a pain, though; the vehicles were not ideal for military purposes. You had to wait for the vehicle to settle on its hydraulic suspension or use one of the sets of steps that appeared only when the vehicle couldn't lower itself because of obstructions under the chassis. Leaping down meant taking a chance on a two-metre drop.

With no weapon mounts, the Marines would have to dismount to engage the enemy, so they planned to get as close as they could without bringing the vehicles into view, then yomp across the remaining distance under cover of their snipers and light support weapons.

Warden sat with Sergeant Milton at a navigation and mapping station going over all the data the colonists had gathered about the ground between the city and North Solar Farm. They were looking for somewhere that they could test the alien weapons in relative safety, far enough from both the city and their destination that the enemy would not know what they were doing.

"There," said Sergeant Milton, pointing at a shallow canyon in the top right of the screen. "It's deep enough to contain any firing and the gradient leading into it should be manageable by the rover."

"It's a little further out of the way than I'd hoped," Warden replied, "but I suppose it's better to be discreet than get into an unexpected firefight."

"There's a cliff face over there, but there's nothing to shield it from either side and no cover for the teams staying with the vehicles. There are rocks by the canyon mouth that we can use as fire positions in case the aliens do find us."

Warden nodded. "Agreed." He used a stylus at the station to enter a change of route on the nav computer and sent it to the driver, a colonist who had volunteered to get them to North Solar Farm. She called back to him to confirm she'd received the updated route, "Why there, though, Captain?"

"It's Lieutenant Warden, actually. We captured some weapons and we want to test them, make sure we can use them before we have to rely on them. The emergency bays don't carry the heavy weapons we'd want for a task like this and we don't have time to wait for the fabricators to produce them. The canyon is a good place to test them away from enemy sight lines and without getting too far away from our attack vector. Can you get us there safely?" he asked.

"Not a problem for the rover, Lieutenant. It can handle the trip easily, even with this load. I'll pass the details to the other rovers," she replied before hailing the drivers in the two trailing vehicles.

Warden turned to Milton. "So, what's your bet on the contents of our haul?"

"I'd eat my socks if we don't have a few railguns there. Two of them are very similar with drum magazines and big shells, but I think one is a grenade launcher and the other is some sort of heavy shotgun. The shells are big, though, so it's either massive explosions or a ridiculous load of pellets," she replied, rocking her hand side to side to indicate the uncertainty about those weapons.

"Railguns would be useful against vehicles or infantry in powered armour. I want the base intact, if possible, but I'm guessing we'll have to flush them out of the buildings once we've taken care of their perimeter personnel," Warden said.

"Yes, sir. The shotgun might be useful for room clearance, but you can't be letting off railguns in a civilian habitat. The rounds will go straight through the walls, and if there are pressurised canisters in the building or one of the team is out of position... It's a recipe for disaster. A grenade launcher would be even worse. Flashbangs only inside, I think," Milton answered.

"We do have a couple of rifles and some personal weapons that might be useful if we've got enough ammunition," mused Warden.

"Possibly. Our carbines are great in close quarters, but if we can use the rifles, we should. I think it's safe to assume they'll have more troops in power armour defending this site, if it really is their forward operating base. The carbines are next to useless against armour – far too risky to rely on them for that – and if we don't want to use our grenade launchers or the alien's heavy weapons inside, armour is going to be a real problem," Milton said.

"If there's evidence of significant armour, we have to do everything we can to overwhelm it before we step inside the buildings. You saw how little damage those armoured scouts took, even after we'd dropped a building on them. Their armour is tougher and lighter than ours. If they have heavier suits for assault troops, we're screwed if we get too close to them."

"Lieutenant? We've reached the canyon," the driver called back over her shoulder.

"Thanks. We'll go on foot from here, shouldn't be more than half an hour," Warden said, turning to the squad. "Masks on, everyone. This far from the habitats, I don't want our performance suffering from the thin atmosphere." The commandos duly attached their breathing gear, checking function and the levels of gas from their HUDs. The gear they had was nothing like a space suit or powered armour but it was more than enough to handle the local environment. It was comforting to know that equipment or air supply failure, even out here, wasn't going to cause them to suffocate in the air of New Bristol. But it would dramatically slow them down.

The driver hit the seal on the cockpit and a thin door slid across, separating the passenger and cargo area from the front of the vehicle. It was a simple way to reduce the amount of atmosphere lost when loading and unloading the vehicle.

Moments later the Marines were on the ground, walking down the shallow incline to the canyon floor. Twenty metres in they found a suitable spot, a bend in the canyon that gave them a good backstop for the weapons to discharge against and sufficient range to keep them safe from ricochets or explosives.

It actually took longer to set up, safety check the weapons and establish a testing protocol than it did to run the tests. They'd recovered a fair amount of ammunition for all the items they had brought along but Warden didn't want to waste too much all the same.

They quickly established that the function of each weapon was nearly identical to their own heavier armaments. The railguns were clearly sniping weapons, with near silent operation and very high target penetration, similar to their own weapons, though they couldn't be exact in a test against a rock wall.

Fired within or at the buildings of the solar farm, the railgun's rounds would punch through the walls and anything that might be on the other side. Warden gave instructions to use these only sparingly, as Milton had suggested. There was a reason nobody had ever produced a railgun capable of burst fire.

The grenade launcher and shotgun were more easily tested. They had anti-armour high explosive grenades as well as fragmentation models, differentiated by colours, just as their own were, although the markings and design were quite different. The shotgun was entirely dull, though it would be useful for clearing rooms of lightly armoured hostiles.

The pistols were high calibre but perfectly usable as backup weapons. All had integral silencers, suggesting that they were intended for stealthy takedowns during the opening stages of an attack. The commandos rarely used pistols because it wasn't necessary to have so much weaponry on a typical deployment but they had their uses.

The alien rifles were full-length assault rifles, not the smaller bullpup carbines the Marines had taken from the armoury. The rounds were a heavier calibre, making them preferable to the carbines, even in close quarters, and they were much more likely to penetrate powered armour than the weapons the Marines carried.

All in all, Warden was pleased. He would have preferred weapons they were familiar with but despite the outward appearances of all of these, the functional designs were similar enough that the Marines weren't going to have any problems changing magazines or firing the weapons. It seemed strange that the first aliens they had encountered were sufficiently similar to humans to be able to use their weapons but he wasn't going to look a gift horse in the mouth and now wasn't the time for serious introspection.

They were back in the rovers within half an hour. Warden and Milton distributed the railguns to the snipers. Each section had at least one Marine who had been through the extensive training required to qualify as a sniper. Lance Corporal Bailey was the senior sniper in A Troop and would lead the team of three snipers, along with their spotters, and the tech specialists who would be using drones to sweep the area.

They gave the grenade launcher and shotgun to the spotters. Without clear targets, their main role was to protect the snipers.

There were only a few assault rifles, so they went to the close quarter specialists, while Milton handed out the alien pistols to as many people as possible. Anyone left with only standard-issue carbines was given more grenades for the underslung launchers. If they encountered powered armour, a grenade would be their best option. Either that or they'd flag the enemy in their HUD and hope the railguns could shoot it through a wall.

Warden looked around the vehicle, checking his team. The Marines looked confident, comfortable. They were as ready as they would ever be.

"Move out," he ordered.

7

As soon as they were underway, Warden reviewed the layout of the solar plant and the settlers' plans of the base with Milton, looking for ways to incorporate the alien weapons into their plan. Together they selected overwatch positions for the snipers, agreed on an approach route and found a rock formation close to the base for the drivers to park behind. Then they polished their plan of attack and issued it to the commandos via their HUDs.

The Marines sat in silence while they reviewed their assigned positions and the lines of attack. The HUDs showed their expected flow through the buildings to clear them, so by the time they reached the vehicles parked, they were ready to do the job.

They piled out of the vehicles without a word, snipers and their support teams breaking away to find positions on a formation of basalt columns. Warden blinked in surprise and spared a glance for Milton, who stood open-mouthed.

"Perfect for snipers," he muttered, watching as the teams climbed the natural terraces and disappeared. The column tops were flat and lacked concealing vegetation but that hardly mattered in this case; the attack would be swift and brutal, and if the snipers were under fire, you couldn't ask for better cover than the hard rock.

While the snipers found their spots, the tech specialists launched their drones, sending them zipping over the columns of rock and down the other side. The drones hugged the ground, skimming low to avoid detection. No bigger than a hummingbird, their bird-like movements would be totally out of place on New Bristol. The indigenous lifeforms generally kept well away from the colonists, and it looked like the local bird equivalents weren't keen on the Marines either. The drones' movements would stand out like a sore thumb to any alien sentries, but it was a risk they had to take.

Warden and Milton split the remaining Marines into two teams while they waited for updated maps to be built from the information returned by the drones. They were watching the video feeds from the drones as some flitted clockwise and some counter-clockwise around the solar plant, scanning everything.

"There," said Warden, zooming in, "that looks like a dropship to me. A large one."

"Seems too big, doesn't it?" said Milton sceptically. "If that was full of troops when it landed, where are they? This camp should be swarming."

"One platoon at the city, a few patrols at other sites." Warden frowned. "There could be two or three platoons here if that thing came down full."

"Unless they carry something else. Vehicles, perhaps? They could have their own colony equipment in there. Do they want to kill us or capture New Bristol and colonise it?"

Warden shrugged. "There's little value in New Bristol, it won't be terraformed for decades, and they don't seem so dissimilar from us that they'd want to call this rock home. Would you come to another solar system and fight a war only to colonise a planet you still had to terraform?"

"No, I wouldn't, but our own history has a lot of similar examples. Maybe aliens are just as stupid as humans?"

"Fair point," conceded Warden with a shrug. "Can't really argue with that. Either way, we can't charge in there unless we know more about their numbers. Agreed?"

"Yes, sir. I have no interest in finding out the hard way that they have three platoons of power armoured troopers just waiting to welcome us."

Warden nodded and briefed the tech specialists, sending new instructions via the HUD. In moments, a dozen more drones were in the air and heading into the camp.

"Now we'll see," murmured Warden as the camp's plan unfolded in his HUD.

He turned his attention back to the drone feeds, but there wasn't anything new. The updated layout showed only superficial changes, like new tool sheds and shifted storage containers, but nothing that presented a challenge for their plan of attack. The only remaining question was the number of enemy troops.

"Milton, get the grenade launchers up on the ridge in case they twig to the drones," he said, advancing on the ridge himself as the sergeant set about reorganising the teams.

Warden climbed the stepped columns, making his way up towards the highest point. He picked a spot a couple of metres down from the peak and hoped he would avoid the sight line of any sentries. Being silhouetted on a ridge was a classic mistake that had been thoroughly drilled out of him in commando training. You could only take so many paintball bruises from the sniping instructors before you got the point about keeping your head down.

The data from the drones and the various displays and map overlays he could access from his HUD were good, he knew, but there was nothing quite like a Mark I eyeball to make a location seem real. He glanced to either side. The snipers waited a little below his position, scanning back and forth, looking for targets.

He took a deep breath and raised his head just far enough above the rock to see the alien spaceship. As he'd seen from the drones, it was large and odd-looking to boot. There were similarities to human ships but it was smoother and less blocky than the Royal Navy's ships, more elegant, somehow.

Dropships didn't need to be attractive beasts and the Navy's certainly weren't, but this one had a somewhat pleasing aesthetic, even if the metal was a strange swirling mix of blues and greens.

But the camouflage hadn't been achieved with mere paint; it was built into the metal of the hull. There was little point camouflaging a dropship designed for rapid entry; it was hardly a subtle affair. Warden shook his head. Alien paint schemes were a puzzle for a quieter day.

There were no sentries around the base and that surprised him. It would be incredibly lax of the enemy commander to have no patrols or sentries guarding their perimeter. Perhaps they were using drones or dumb sensors? Maybe they had launched an attack elsewhere?

"Anyone got an update for me? Come on, people, give me something," he said, clenching his fist, trying to keep the frustration from his voice. He needed to know what was going on here, where the enemy were and how many of them were running around. If they didn't get something soon, they'd have to push on regardless. The captain had given him a job to do and the colonists expected results. He gave the solar plant one last look and then began to descend the steps of rock.

"Grenade launchers are in place, sir," said Milton. "We're three hundred metres from the first building we can use as cover. Do you want to move in now or wait to confirm numbers?"

"We'll give the techs two more minutes, then we move. We'll just have to risk it."

Milton nodded and they moved to their respective teams, walking them towards the side of the rock formation. The drones had advanced well into the plant by the time Milton's and Warden's teams reached the last of the rocks. Any further and they would be in the open terrain between the rocks and the first buildings.

<Anyone else?> Warden asked across the HUD.

Cooke, the tech specialist for Section 1 responded, sending his report to Warden and Milton only.

<Negative, sir. We've flagged the buildings the drones have cleared but we can't get into the central structure, so we expect the enemy are in

there if they're here at all. No sentries or automated defences. The drop-ship is cold; engines haven't been fired recently, the ship is at atmospheric temperature, and there are no signs of active scanning. We have drones at all the breaching points. We're ready to go. If there's no immediate contact when you breach, we can send the drones in so they can scout the interior. The structure is like a bunker, and it's blocking our scans, but the interior walls probably aren't any more solid than they were in Ashton. There's some accommodation in there for a few people and storage space, so plenty of room to put their barracks and armour in there>

<Understood> replied Warden. He switched to the public channel. <Overwatch, we're moving out in thirty seconds. Any enemy contact, fire at will> he ordered.

He glanced at the time on his HUD, counting down, "Three, two, one. Go!" he called as he broke into a run. Even wearing breathers, the thin air took its toll; without them, the three hundred metre dash would have been a real lung-buster. Warden's heart pounded in his chest as he broke free of the safety offered by the basalt.

Section 2 followed behind him, eyes on the base, everyone looking for the first sign of trouble. The ground was flat and hard, no dips to dive into or boulders to shelter behind. They were horribly exposed to enemy fire.

<All clear, Lieutenant, no sign> sent Bailey when Warden reached the halfway point.

<Noted> he responded <Don't let up the pace>

They skidded to a halt behind the first building, not much more than a low concrete ridge topped with thin metal walls and a roof. It wasn't the best cover but it was long enough that both teams could shelter behind it while they caught their breath. Warden took a moment to check the drone feeds. Still no sign of enemy movement.

It was beginning to irritate him. Where were the bastards? He would almost rather see sentries and some defensive positions, if only to confirm that they were in the right place. He checked the bio-readouts for his team; heart rates were almost settled, so he moved up from his crouch and made another run.

The teams split up now, filtering through the buildings in smaller groups, double-checking the drones' information as they went, bursting through doors and checking for concealed sentries.

They quickly made their way to the main building, coordinating their approach so that they hit both entrances at the same time. The building was squat and ugly, another bunker with a single storey above ground and more space below.

Marine X drew his standard-issue pistol and fitted a suppressor as Harrington reached for the door handle. Locked. Harrington made space for Fletcher, who pressed a mechanical pick against the handle. The machine buzzed briefly then the lock clicked open, and Fletcher stepped back. Warden shouldered his weapon and checked the grenade launcher. The silenced pistol would make short work of an unarmoured alien but wouldn't dent power armour.

The door came open at Harrington's touch to reveal a small room with a concrete staircase descending into the basement on the left and another set of doors opposite. To the right were benches and coats as well as breathing gear. Still no guards.

Warden wanted to check on Milton at the other end of the building, but she didn't need his help and wouldn't thank him for distracting her. Milton's target, the main entrance, had a door for workers and a large roller shutter for forklift access. No carbine fire, so no serious contact yet. Warden nodded to himself and signalled his team to move in.

Marine X, or Ten, as he was known to the Marines, slipped into the room. Four other Marines followed, silenced pistols at the ready, to clear the way as quietly as possible.

The plans suggested the lower floor was mostly storage, but Warden wasn't going to leave any part of the base unchecked, no matter how unlikely the enemy's presence. The colonists' inventory listed a workshop and dozens of containers full of solar panel spare parts and other equipment. That didn't mean the aliens hadn't barracked more soldiers down here or filled the place with weapons.

Marine X, Harrington and Fletcher headed down the staircase to the lower level as per the plan, so Warden ordered the bulk of the section forward. Lee and Campbell took the lead with their suppressed pistols at the ready. They were backed by colleagues carrying the more robust alien weapons. Two more quietly opened the doors and the lead Marines crept forward.

Like the offices at the hydroponics hall, the floor space was divided by thin partition walls, some of which had windows into corridors. There was an office area to their right, every wall of which was glazed along the upper half. No aliens to be seen, nothing to be heard.

Warden sent two Marines to check the offices. Lee and Campbell advanced down a corridor to the left and Warden hunkered down in the front room to watch the feed from their HUDs. They came to a windowed door and Lee risked a quick glance inside. A canteen.

Though Lee had only looked through the window for a fraction of a second, they replayed the video via the HUD. Three aliens were inside, two with wings eating at a table, the third at a coffee machine, waiting for it to dispense. It had scaly skin, completely different from the winged snipers'. None of them wore armour. Campbell sent a query to Warden.

The reply was a simple confirmation: <Execute>

Lee and Campbell opened the door and strode into the room bold as brass. Nothing flashy, nothing dramatic, not like in a movie. These soldiers weren't expecting an attack; they hadn't even posted guards.

The winged snipers barely had time to react before Lee's rounds punched into their skulls, one looking up in surprise over the slumping shoulder of his colleague before his head rocked back, shattered. The coffee-drinker slumped to the ground with two bullets in the spine and one in the back of the head. Warden nodded, grimly pleased. Textbook and swift.

He updated the kills on the HUD and sent a message to Milton. Her response showed her team on the north side of the bunker. They had found a barracks but no aliens and no sign that they had yet been detected.

Warden could imagine her contempt for their enemy's lax attitude. Not that anyone wanted a fair fight, but Milton would surely also be experiencing the strange mix of embarrassment and pity that

Warden felt. Then he shook his head. Bollocks to that; these bastards had invaded New Bristol and killed colonists and Marines alike. They deserved no sympathy.

Warden ordered Milton to hold as long as possible while his section made their way through this floor towards her and Marine X cleared the basement. Milton acknowledged while Warden checked in with Marine X, who merely confirmed they had found nothing of interest. They were heading towards the north wall where there was a staircase that would bring them out on the other side of the barracks area.

Warden updated the HUD and issued new orders. Section 1 would advance slowly and check each room, Marine X would come up from the basement, and together they would clear the barracks area after rendezvousing with Milton's section.

The bunker had multiple rooms, some small and private, some larger bunks. They were probably only used when the colonists were moving across New Bristol from site to site or doing a maintenance run. There hadn't been many people stationed here day to day as solar plants didn't need much care and attention.

Terraformers liked to build plenty of capacity into their infrastructure. When the terraforming was done, population growth would consume any surplus and if the weather or atmospheric conditions changed, it was always good to have a backup. Bunker-like storm shelters were also popular, as was excess capacity in everything from food production to sleeping quarters to energy plants.

Warden was ready to declare the area clear, already heading back to join his section, when a door opened and a huge alien stepped into the corridor. Eight feet tall, heavily muscled and with scales for skin, the thing had to duck its head to avoid the ceiling. It stood frozen for a moment, caught between Warden and the Marines, nobody able to shoot in the narrow corridor.

Then it roared and took a step towards the Marines. Warden charged, pistol discarded and knife out, reaching for the alien's head with one hand while the other swept round to chop out the beast's throat.

But the alien was fast, much faster than Warden would have believed possible. It whipped around and batted the knife away with one huge fist, then hurled the other at Warden's head. The lieutenant ducked, narrowly avoiding the blow, but the beast was canny and cool, and a heavy cross caught him across the jaw, knocking him back and messing with his vision. Before he could move, another blow caught him and sent him sprawling, sliding along the corridor on his back.

As he lay there, dazed and half-senseless, he heard a long series of sharp pops. Then the alien slumped back against the wall and slid to the floor.

The Marines hurried forward and Campbell helped Warden to his feet.

"You okay, sir? Ya took a couple of good shots to the bonce, there."

Warden shook his head, blinking as his vision cleared, then spat blood on the floor. Campbell pressed Warden's knife and pistol into his hands.

"Mebbe next time ya let us shoot the buggers first, eh, sir? Save the fisticuffs for when we get home."

The lieutenant nodded, rubbing his jaw.

Then the HUD lit up with a message from Milton.

<Contact>

8

Milton swore. Profusely. They had been approaching the barracks, as quiet as mice and as good as gold when it had all gone to shit. A squad of alien troopers had spewed from the room like a bad choice at a buffet. These ones wore body armour and they all carried the powerful rifles that seemed to be their main weapon. They might not all have shoes or trousers on, but that didn't mean they weren't a serious threat.

The Marines had been forced back, abandoning the forward positions in favour of not being cut to ribbons. Milton hunkered down behind a storage locker, hoping it didn't contain anything sensitive to high-velocity impacts. *Mustn't grumble,* she thought. The locker door was nice and flat, so at least her back was comfortable.

The corridor she was supposed to have taken, the one that was only inches past her left shoulder, was currently a horizontal hailstorm of death. That was a bit of a problem. She had to admit that they were in a spot of bother. Milton looked to her left, where Justine Barber was crouching on the other side of the corridor.

Barber let out a huge sigh as if to express just how bored she was at having to wait her turn. She put her rifle in her lap, drew a pistol, passed it into her left hand and twisted at the waist. The suppressor was attached and she poked the barrel around the corner and pulled the trigger, randomly returning fire until the magazine was empty. Barber looked up at Sergeant Milton and shrugged.

It was worth a try, Milton supposed. It was certainly better than sticking your head out. They were at a T-junction, and the wall opposite the corridor was thoroughly peppered with bullet holes. On the plus side, if the aliens kept up that rate of fire, they would have to run out of ammunition soon. Surely?

Milton switched her gaze to her HUD, checked the status of her team and noted that, although the aliens had surprised them, only a few had picked up flesh wounds. It wasn't her best day as a Commando but it could have been a whole lot more painful.

<What's the situation?> sent Warden, the text flowing into Milton's HUD.

<Bit of a pickle, sir. They pushed hard and we only got a couple before we had to fall back. The aliens have the better positions and an apparently unlimited supply of ammunition. Any chance you can lend a hand?> Milton replied via the HUD, flagging the problematic control points she needed to clear on the map.

<Let me check with my secretary; I'm not sure what's on today's calendar. Can I call you back after lunch?>

<I'd prefer it if you could make it a little earlier>

<Smoke me a kipper then and we'll see you for breakfast>

"The Lieutenant is on the way," said Milton to Barber and Mitchell, shouting to be heard over the din, "he wants smoked kippers for breakfast so let's stop buggering about, shall we?" Milton pulled a smoke grenade from her pouch. Barber copied her as Mitchell readied his rifle, standing up and turning to face the corridor.

Milton and Barber threw their grenades and a second later smoke began to pour into the corridor. Mitchell leaned around the corner, fired a couple of bursts into the smoke, then ducked back. *That should give the buggers something to think about while Warden brings his group to bear.*

Milton messaged the rest of her team, telling them to keep their heads down until backup arrived. Sporadic bursts of fire cracked nearby, but the aliens hadn't returned fire down the smoke-filled corridor yet. Maybe they were waiting for the smoke to clear.

Milton turned around to her right and inspected lockers on the wall. Access was by key card, so she tried the one she'd taken off the enemy. None of the locks responded so they were probably meant for specific personnel or roles like engineering crew. Her pistol didn't have any problems opening the lock, though. These weren't safes, after all.

Inside she found boxes of spare parts. Barber looked at her quizzically and fired a short burst down the corridor while Milton rooted around in the boxes. She found what she was looking for and crouched by the corner again, facing the corridor.

The object Milton lobbed sailed into the smoke and bounced across the floor. There was a break in the firing around them and they could hear it rolling down the corridor. They heard footsteps and a few thuds. Someone had hit the deck. Barber grinned at her and Milton winked. She waited a couple of seconds then threw another.

There was more frantic scrabbling from the far end of the corridor so she bounced the third off a wall, high up, hoping it would find an open doorway. More shouting and a burst of fire. She lobbed one more, but they were wise to the game, now, and instead of dodging away they simply fired back, shooting indiscriminately down the corridor.

The arrival of the fifth fake grenade must have caught them by surprise when it exploded in their midst. It certainly sounded like someone was in pain.

"Nice one, Sarge," Mitchell said with a grin and Barber gave a thumbs up. At least one enemy trooper was down, groaning at the end of the corridor. Milton lobbed a few more of her fake grenades then another smoke grenade. Then she hefted her rifle, listening for the sound of enemy movement.

At the other end of the barracks, Warden pulled the trigger and stitched a neat line across the exposed back of an alien trooper. He switched targets but the next one was already down, so he marked the point as safe on the HUD and saw that two more were already cleared.

<Milton, how are you doing?> he sent.

<We're all good, sir. Quieter here, now. They seem to have other things on their minds>

Warden checked the HUD, examining the positions of his troops and the enemy. The Marines now had the aliens boxed in on two sides now, but the barracks could hold, what, another dozen troops or so? They could press forward and find out the hard way, but that wasn't his only option.

<Are you in position?> he asked. The only response was an affirmative ping, the silent method used by commandos waiting stealthily to attack.

<Milton, it's time to invite our guests to the buffet. Let's make sure they get the message, in three, two, one>

Noise erupted around the barracks, as both Milton's team and Warden's directed fire at the points controlled by the aliens. Bursts of fire hammered the doors and hurtled down the corridors. No sane alien would poke its head out while that cacophony was going on.

Harrington and Fletcher advanced from the lower level, their guns trained on two targets. Marine X was between them, his attention on a third alien. All three of the enemy were shooting, their attention entirely on the hail of bullets that was suppressing them. Big mistake.

Marine X closed with his target, his hand clamping around the forehead and the blade of his knife sinking smoothly between the vertebrae in its neck. He wrenched the knife from side to side, completely severing the spinal column, then withdrew it.

On either side of him, there were soft coughs as Harrington and Fletcher discharged their responsibilities, their suppressed weapons inaudible over the exchanges of gunfire between the aliens and the Marines.

None of the aliens noticed until it was too late for them to react. The weapons of Marine X, Harrington and Fletcher dealt with five more enemy troopers before the aliens finally realised they were surrounded. Warden watched through his HUD and as soon as the aliens began to turn he ordered a full assault.

They all rushed forward, converging under cover of fire and overwhelming the remaining half-dozen aliens in seconds. A few additional shots were put into still thrashing bodies to make sure, and then there was deathly quiet. Warden stood breathing heavily for a few moments as he surveyed the scene and nodded in satisfaction.

"Commandos, log your kills, we need numbers," he ordered, and a steady flow of data began to come in via his HUD. Twenty-eight, in total, since entering the base.

Warden switched channels. <Overwatch, any activity> he sent <or any movement from the dropship?>

<No, sir. All quiet on the southern front. No sensor sweeps from the ship, engines are not powering up. The techs have got their main drones up, and there's nothing at the nearest outposts either> came the response from Wilson.

Warden acknowledged the updates and walked over to the barracks, issuing orders as he went.

<Overwatch, maintain alert and keep an eye on that dropship. Anyone with alien hardware, get yourselves into cover as close to the dropship as possible. We need to breach it as soon as we can, and I don't want any surprises coming out of it>

Warden surveyed the carnage in the barracks room. Maybe the aliens were nocturnal? They might come from a planet with a hostile daylight environment or predators. Or a variety of planets, perhaps. He'd spotted at least four types of aliens so far.

"Check the lockers, search the bodies. We're looking for their dropship pilots so we can find their access cards or whatever they use," he barked to the commandos standing around in the barracks.

Milton issued the same order to those near the individual bedrooms: look for a pilot or officers, bring everything you find back to the barracks room for sorting.

"Marine X – did you find an armoury downstairs by any chance? I don't see anything but personal weapons up here," Warden asked.

Ten grinned broadly. "Yes, sir. Want me to show you?"

He nodded and followed the Marine down the nearby staircase, signalling a few nearby commandos to join them.

"You might want to get someone to count the dead down here, sir," Ten said as they descended the staircase.

"What? I didn't hear anything. How many was it and why didn't you say before now?"

"I kept it quiet, as ordered, sir. That's what you pay me for," replied the unrepentant Marine.

"Point of fact, Marine X," said Warden pointedly, "you're still serving at Her Majesty's pleasure for that incident on Arcturus 4, so you're not being paid at all. You have to complete another four deployments before you earn a salary again."

Marine X shrugged as if it wasn't a big deal. "True," he conceded. "And I didn't log the kills, too busy. Sorry, sir," he added, not looking even slightly sorry.

"Use your bloody HUD next time," snapped Warden, "that's what it's for and you might have needed more backup," he said, trying to get the Marine to understand. Marine X might be serving a penal sentence for his earlier breaches of military conduct but he was still a valuable commando.

Aside from discipline issues, Marine X was probably the most skilled and dangerous commando in Captain Atticus's command, maybe even the battalion. But that didn't explain why he had been deployed to the front line instead of serving out his sentence somewhere safe and boring. Warden shook his head. Marine X was an enigma for another day.

Besides, in this situation, Warden couldn't afford to lose any Marines early, certainly not before they had an active cloning bay again. He doubted his point would make it into Ten's brain, though. The man was incorrigible. Warden had heard that the only person who had been killed more times in action was Captain Atticus himself.

"Sorry, sir. Harrington and Fletcher can count them, though. They went past the ones I found when they joined me on the staircase, so they know where all the bodies are," said Ten cheerfully.

"They weren't with you? They were your backup!" Warden snapped again, now thoroughly pissed off.

"I told them to hang back and cover me. No point risking them if I ran across any problems."

Warden sighed. There were good reasons why Ten was an administrative and disciplinary nightmare but you couldn't argue with his demonstrable and obvious bravery. The man would much rather die himself than let a fellow Marine take a fatality.

Warden made a note in his HUD to review the Marine's progress through this ground floor later. In most cases, commanders didn't have the time or need to review individual troopers' feeds. Penal Marine X's videos, however, were always educational and Warden wasn't afraid to admit that he could learn from them and improve his future performance.

"Here it is, sir," said Ten, pointing to a large storage cage. There were two dead aliens outside it. One was in fairly normal body armour and had been carrying what Warden was fairly sure was one of the combat shotguns they had tested earlier. Its head lolled at an obscene angle, a huge gash across its throat. Any more and it would have been decapitated.

The other was more of a surprise. It was wearing power armour. Warden looked at it, then glanced at Marine X, who wore a beatific expression that seemed to say, 'Who, sir? Me, sir? I ain't done nuffin.' He could almost hear it in Ten's south London accent. Clearly, he should have called for backup to deal with this target as he wasn't carrying anything that should have been used to engage a trooper in powered armour except grenades.

"Why didn't you request backup or use a grenade?" Warden asked incredulously. If he hadn't seen the psychologists reports, he would have thought the man insane.

Ten shrugged again. "Looked like this was their armoury, sir. Didn't think you'd want me to destroy any of their weapons, what with us not having anything that's much use."

Warden looked at the corpse again. He wasn't even going to ask how Marine X had managed it; he'd just watch the HUD feed later.

Milton isn't going to believe this, he thought.

Ten dragged the smaller alien away from the storage cage door so that it could open fully. It hung ajar, a broken lock dangling from the bolt. Warden went inside and looked around. The space was large, about the size of a standard shipping container.

There were several large crates secured with electronic locks and the shelves had been neatly stacked with small arms. He nodded thoughtfully; there was probably enough in here to equip all the remaining men and women of the commando with the aliens' superior weapons.

He inspected the lock on one of the crates then turned back to Ten who was kneeling by the heavily armoured alien, rifling through its pouches. He found something and held it up with a triumphant grin, standing and walking to the doorway to toss it to Warden.

A key card, alien in appearance but entirely the same concept they used on their restricted munitions. If you broke open a crate of RMSC grenade launchers, explosive charges would destroy the contents and put you at considerable risk. It wouldn't surprise him if the aliens took similar measures and, if their technology had developed based on that found on a Lost Ark ship, it might be identical.

Warden wasn't a historian, so he had no idea if self-destruct protocols were in use during the period of the Lost Ark missions. They didn't even know which ship these aliens had encountered; it could have been one of the first lost or the most recent.

He motioned for Marine X to stand back, just in case there were any additional security measures and using the card went wrong, then he waved the key card in front of the dull, red lock on the case. It went green, and there was a series of pops and clicks as the locks opened. Gingerly, he lifted the lid, as if gentleness itself might stop it exploding.

The crate contained three of the huge combat shotguns.

"What do you think, Marine X – useful for boarding their dropship?"

"Works for me, but I wouldn't use them around any engineering equipment or the bridge."

"Worried something might explode?"

"No, I just assumed you wanted the dropship intact so we could get to the ship in orbit and deal with it, sir."

Warden stared at him for a moment. *Shit,* he thought. He hadn't thought that far ahead. The aliens must have a ship in orbit and he had no idea what its capabilities were or what sort of threat it posed. The aliens' weapons and armour were recognisable but significantly different to models from Sol and its colonies. The dropship itself looked substantially different and what did that say about the rest of their fleet?

What would their orbital ship be like? Did it have orbital bombardment capacity or was it a troop carrier? Was it a scout ship or a battleship, or maybe a capital ship? It could even be based on an Ark ship; the earliest models had hangar bays for launching smaller craft like this dropship. Some orbital ships could land planetside but most used shuttles and dropships to deploy personnel and equipment, whether military or civilian.

"Shit," muttered Warden. They couldn't leave the damned thing up there; it could launch a second invasion or, worse, simply bombard the planet from orbit. Marine X was right; they had to take the dropship intact and get into orbit as soon as possible.

"Yes, well, if we can work out how to pilot it, you're right," Warden said.

"Probably got an autopilot for returning to the ship, unless we're deeply unlucky."

Warden nodded, setting the question to one side. "Right, help me open up the rest of these crates. We need to know what's worth taking up and what we should leave here."

"Right ho, sir."

They set about counting the weapons and classifying them, entering them into the HUD to create an updated list of all weapons and munitions available to the local RMSC. The Marines' weapons all reported ammunition usage so that commanders could monitor their units' combat readiness. A warning would pop up in a Marine's

HUD when they hit key stages, such as a 50% ammunition depletion or exhaustion of all anti-aircraft rockets.

The alien weapons wouldn't feed data back to the Marines but, long ago, some bright young HUD interface designer had decided the commandos might need to avail themselves of captured weapons to continue fighting. As a result, the facility to manually record data had been in the HUD since before Warden joined up.

They'd gained some more grenade launchers, a couple of rocket launchers that he guessed were for anti-aircraft use and some more sniper rifles, both standard and railgun. They wouldn't take the latter because railguns could easily open a ship to vacuum if you found the right spot; grenades and rocket launchers were similarly problematic.

Fortunately, they also found plenty of combat rifles, which would be far more effective than the Marines' standard carbines, especially if they encountered heavy resistance from powered armour.

"Need a really big knife?" Warden said, holding up an enormous alien combat knife as he turned to show it to Marine X.

Ten grinned and produced an identical knife with a flourish that made it materialize in his fist as if plucked from this air. "Already found 'em, sir."

"Ohhh-kay," Warden replied, "you don't think they're a bit much, maybe?"

"Yeah, bigger than you really need, but flip the thumb switch and give it a go," said Ten with a glint in his eye.

Thumb switch? Warden looked down at the knife and saw a depression under the hilt, cunningly concealed by the metal of the cross guard so you couldn't accidentally activate it. He held the knife up and pushed his thumb into the button. Immediately the knife began to hum and gently vibrate, shimmering faintly in the dim light of the cage.

"Hmmm. Well, that's a new one on me. Worked out what it does yet?" Warden asked.

Ten nodded and pointed at the side of the cage to Warden's left. There was a neat circular hole as if someone had cut through the wire of the cage and one of the metal supports with an arc welder.

Warden stepped over and put the edge of the knife against the wire; it parted as easily as you'd slice a tomato. The knife barely slowed as he dragged it through the solid steel frame of the cage.

"It only stays on as long as you keep your thumb in the hole," explained Ten. "A dead man's handle in case you drop it on your leg while it's still buzzing. It's bloody useless if you're trying to creep up on a sentry, but with one of these you could make short work of him, even if he was in power armour."

At that comment, Warden looked back at the box he'd pulled the knife from. There were three empty slots, so it looked like Ten hadn't got his knife in time to use it on the sentries outside. And he had taken two, for some reason. Warden sighed, but if anyone was going to find a use for two huge knives that could cut through power armour, it would be Marine X. Warden decided to leave him to it as long as he didn't catch him playing around with it in the company mess.

"Find anything else we might want for the boarding party?" Warden asked.

"Yeah. Have a butcher's at these," said Ten, pointing to a medium-sized crate he'd opened.

It was full of large pistols with long, thick barrels. Warden picked one up and ejected the magazine. Unloaded, as you would hope. They checked the shelves and found the bullets that fit the weapon.

The grip seemed to fit his hand reasonably well, and he aimed it, squeezing the trigger until it discharged a round. The flak armoured alien corpse bucked with the impact. The gun was remarkably quiet, which meant it had a high-quality suppression system as well as subsonic ammunition.

"Nice," he said, passing the weapon to Ten who promptly fired a couple more shots into each alien.

"Yeah, not much cop against the power armour, but they're better than our pistols all the same," Ten shrugged, "and if you're hoping to take the orbital ship against superior numbers, these would help to start things quietly."

"Okay, let's get everything upstairs and get this assault underway. I don't want to hang about here longer than necessary," Warden ordered. He told Milton to send down some more bodies so they could get their haul up top quickly. The goods elevators were still working so it didn't take long to move the weapons and begin distributing them to the eager Marines.

"New plan," Warden said to Milton before outlining his concerns about a ship in orbit. The sergeant listened impassively then nodded.

"Makes sense," she admitted, although it was clear she didn't really like the plan. "How do you want to do it?"

"Dropship first," said Warden as they watched the alien weapons being distributed.

There was still no sign of life in the enemy dropship; it was entirely possible that there weren't any personnel aboard to guard it, but they wouldn't be taking any risks. Milton had found two aliens whose lockers had held what appeared to be flight suits. They had key cards and their personal weapons were pistols. The fact they had been assigned individual bedrooms and appeared to be officers strongly supported the conclusion that they were the dropship's flight crew.

They were ready. Warden gave the signal and the team loped across the open ground to the dropship.

He leaned against the outer hull, near what looked like the main door. It had been agreed that Marine X would lead the breaching party, a small group of Marines who had all taken the specialist courses in stealth operations. Marine X had served long enough that he had done most of the courses available at one time or another, but the younger recruits were always more specialised.

Warden glanced once more at Milton and the other NCOs. No sign of doubt in their eyes.

"Breach!" he ordered.

9

Ten had strapped one of the alien knives to his chest for easy access. It was ungainly but the ability to penetrate armour was a significant advantage over his standard-issue Fairbairn-Sykes commando dagger. He also carried two of the alien pistols and a number of flashbang grenades. He took a deep breath and nodded at Fletcher, who swiped the pilot's access card over the lock. It went green, and the doors at the top of the ramp slipped noiselessly into the walls.

There was no ambush waiting for them, just a typical loading bay. A small all-terrain vehicle sat on the floor with a few lockers and storage cages but there were no enemy personnel or automated defences to be seen.

Ten climbed the ramp, a pistol in each hand, checking the bay properly before signalling his team. He made his way to the personnel door and looked around. Some ships had maps at important junctions to help visitors, but he hadn't really expected them on an invading dropship. *Pity*, he thought, *would have been handy.*

Their goal was to neutralise the crew as quickly as possible. They might not know the internal layout of the dropship but they knew where the entrances, engines and cockpit were. The ramp had come down facing the nose of the ship, and the cockpit was somewhere above and behind them as a result. There were two more ramps on the port and starboard side of the ship, further back towards the engines.

As the pilots were dead, the cockpit was probably empty but two Marines were tasked to clear it anyway while the rest headed for the central area of the ship. They planned to dominate each junction and clear every space they passed, looking for crew quarters, engineering section and the mess hall – the most likely places to find the crew.

Ten didn't really know why ships had engineering sections. It seemed redundant since aside from pilots, weapons crew and medics, almost everyone on a ship of any size was an engineer, mechanic or technician of some sort. They were the majority of the crew, so they were everywhere.

Still, as soon as a ship got large enough, there was always a section that was referred to as 'engineering' and that usually held only an array of displays and chairs, much like every other position on the ship. Only the very largest ships could support an actual engineering bay for producing spare parts and repairing portable systems. Smaller ships simply carried a few spares for emergency replacements.

Yet since the crews who maintained the ships tended to hold affection for them, it was likely that the aliens had left some personnel on the ship rather than taking everyone to the solar plant.

The ramp access room's only personnel exit faced away from the cockpit. There was also a goods lift that went up to the next deck. Ten elected to take the lift, on his own, and start clearing the next deck. As soon as they had cleared the front of the ship, Warden would move the rest of the force into position and storm the ship, should a firefight ensue.

Ten got into the lift, located the control and signalled the rest of his team to proceed. As they flowed silently into the next room, Ten pressed the button and the lift smoothly ascended one deck. He found himself in a large room similar to the ramp room but with displays on each wall and a series of desks and chairs before each display. There was a command chair in the middle, but all the seats were empty.

"Like the bloody *Mary Celeste,*" muttered Ten as he looked around.

This was a tactical room for directing ground forces rather than ship-to-ship combat. Each display showed a different view of New Bristol. Some were showing feeds from orbit, so either the aliens had more ships or they had left satellites in geostationary orbit. Ten pinged that information to Warden. The Marines might not be able to scan objects in orbit at the moment, but this was exactly the sort of information that would keep Warden off his back while he got on with the real work.

None of the displays showed the ship's interior and Ten was no technical specialist. He could pilot a drone, in a pinch, but the specialists who knew him would never have offered him their kit. *Probably worried I'd break their toys*, he thought. Playing with the controls seemed like an easy way to disclose his presence on the dropship to the crew or the ships in orbit, so instead he concentrated on his core skillset – sneaking around and killing things.

The TacRoom had three exits: port, starboard and toward the engines. He went through the nearest exit on the port side. He was fine with port and starboard; it was planetside and orbit that got confusing. Planetside could be the top of the ship or the bottom, depending on the ship's orientation; it changed if the ship moved.

For now, though, up and down were fine, and there weren't any Naval crew around to give him grief about his sense of direction in space. They always seemed to know which way the planets were, though he was buggered if he could work out how. He'd been in the brig more than once after explaining to some gobby rating or other how little he cared about the matter.

Ten opened the door and checked to his right. Nothing but an empty wall, as he had expected. The front of the dropship was sloped, so this upper deck ended further back on the ship than the lower one which held the cockpit. The left was clear and he padded down it, focussing on the slightest sound that might give away an enemy presence. Past the TacRoom was a door on the left. No window.

Ten eased the handle down and stepped into the room. It was pitch black, but a dim light came on the moment the door opened more than a crack. At first, he started, thinking there might be someone in there, but it was a small, empty cabin. Clearly a space for an officer with an automatic light.

The corridor ran along the inside of the hull so there were no rooms on the port side. He had two more doors to check before he reached the end of this section. More empty cabins. At the corner, he thought he heard a noise. Crouched, he tried to relax, ready to spring into action.

He gave it thirty seconds but nothing came around the corner, so he raised his weapon and leant out to peer into the next corridor. Nothing. The short length of corridor was an empty T-junction, leading aft and across to the cabins on the starboard side of this deck. There was no sign of anyone to aft when he rounded that corner either.

Ten was in the zone, aware of everything around him and moving like a buttered cat, alert to any noise and ready for action. He checked the cabins, still searching for crew members. The first was empty and he was moving faster now, taking more risks. If the rooms were empty, noise hardly mattered; if they were occupied, even the quietest opening of the door would give him away. The second cabin was also empty.

The last door opened before he could reach it. An alien stuck its head out and looked aft.

Mistake, thought Ten with a wicked grin. *I'm behind you.*

He fired two rounds into the back of the alien's skull, and it crumpled to the ground. Dirty overalls and a data slate marked it as an engineer and something about the form seemed feminine. Ten gritted his teeth. He preferred not to kill women, but this was an invasion force and, male or female, they had come looking for him.

Still, he wasn't likely to tell anyone at a family get-together about this not-so-glorious moment. Someone always wanted to know why he didn't simply knock out the bad guys and arrest them as if he were some kind of intergalactic policeman. Perhaps he should use some kind of multi-purpose sonic device to incapacitate them before delivering a stern lecture about modern ethical standards.

He headed aft, following the short corridor between two food storage rooms. He took a guess at the next space and was proved right, a mess hall. Nothing large, nothing fancy. You kept things simple if you didn't want crockery flying around when the ship manoeuvred near a planet. Or, of course, when your dropship went through re-entry.

His musings were abruptly interrupted by the two aliens in coveralls who were waiting for him. They looked up as he entered, bearing expressions that went quickly from puzzled, to surprised, to terrified as they realised he wasn't the colleague who'd just gone to its room, he wasn't their species, and he was aiming a weapon at them. The gun spat six times, and he had loaded a new magazine before they finished slumping to the table they'd been eating at.

Where there's a mess, there's a galley, and, sure enough, there was a hatch in the opposite wall. Ten checked it, but there was no sign of a cook. He passed through the only door out of the mess and checked the galley. Empty. On a ship this size, the crew probably just heated their own meals and the troops weren't on it long enough to care.

There were toilet facilities next door and then another goods lift with a ladder next to it. Ten liked ladders; they were silent, they never failed, and they were easy to use in zero-g. Ten sent an update to the rest of his team then took the lift, since the crew wouldn't be surprised when it moved.

Most of the ship was empty, just the engine compartment left to clear. The team had killed two more of the engineering crew and managed to do it silently.

Ten reached the lower deck as the rest of the team came around the corner. They flowed through the two doors, half a team to each, without stopping to greet him. Ten following along behind.

The first room was somewhat unexpected. Large and almost the width of the ship, there were exits to the boarding ramps on either side. More surprising were the pods that lined the fore and aft walls. None of them had expected that.

They also hadn't really expected four power-armoured enemy troopers. The first Marine through each door was riddled with bullets the moment they reached the centre of the room. The rest dived for cover.

Bringing up the rear on the starboard side, Ten saw the hitherto successful mission collapse into pandemonium. The first Marine from his group was pummelled to the ground by shots that struck between his shoulder blades, punched through his chest and ruined the decking below. He was dead before he knew what hit him.

Ten knew, though. The room was almost double height and above the doors was a balcony. The enemy were up there, and they had battle rifles. While his team dived for cover and desperately searched for the source of the shots, Ten dashed to his left and up the steep metal staircase to the balcony, yanking two grenades from his webbing as he went.

Halfway up the stairs, he lobbed the grenades onto the balcony then crouched and waited, eyes closed. The grenades detonated with a deafening crack and what would have been a blinding flash if he hadn't been prepared for it.

He dashed up the remaining steps, spinning as he did and twitching the trigger of his pistol. His ears were ringing, and his shots were wild, but he emptied the magazine, steadying his aim as he moved. Press the enemy hard, when they least expect it. Soldiers don't expect to meet an enemy who simply charges them head on, bringing the fight right to them.

So that's what Ten did.

The first alien, shocked by the flashbangs and the shots ringing from its armour, hunched back as if it were seriously threatened. Maybe it was hurt. More likely it was only disoriented, stunned by the grenades and surprised by the pistol rounds striking its armour.

Ten dropped his pistol, drew both knives and thumbed the mechanisms. They purred to life and he slashed them at the alien's chest, left then right. The blades skittered across the armour, screeching and jumping as the alien tried to stumble clear of its attacker. Closer now, inside the alien's reach, Ten struck again. A blade bit home, driving through a weak point in the armpit, and the monster roared in pain. Ten twisted the handle, hands suddenly wet with blood.

The other knife slammed into the alien's hip joint, an instinctive strike that would have been fatal to a human. Ten pushed hard, both knives twisting as he drove the alien back. It fell, screaming behind its mask, and Ten let it go, the blades still in place. He caught the alien's rifle as it fell and spun it round, shouldering it smoothly as he dropped to one knee. The aliens were recovering, the effects of the grenades already fading, but they were slow, far too slow.

Ten's grin was manic as the rifle bucked against his shoulder. He gritted his teeth, muscles straining to keep the muzzle climb under control. He forced the gun down, fighting for control, envious of the aliens in their servo-assisted powered-armour. And then the second alien's faceplate collapsed and the head disappeared, blown away by the relentless attack.

But it had taken too long. The two aliens on the other side of the bay turned towards him and all he could do was move. He grabbed the collar of the alien who was busy dying from knife wounds and dragged it upright. Crouched behind the power armour as bullets began to slam into the back of the suit, Ten snatched something from the alien's belt with a feral grin.

A second later, the alien grenade exploded, and he was punched backwards, the power armour collapsing on top of him. He ripped the shattered HUD from his eyes, rolled the alien off him and grabbed the rifle. Lying on his back, he fired bursts into the heads of the remaining aliens as they tried to regain their feet.

The rifle clicked, magazine exhausted, and suddenly the only sound was a sort of wordless scream. Ten drew breath and realised it was him screaming. The aliens were gone, their shattered bodies sprawled across the walkways, and he was alone in a room full of corpses.

For a moment he lay there, breathing heavily, the rifle's smoking barrel resting on his boots. Then he kicked himself to his feet and grabbed a knife. Powered armour didn't always need a living host and Ten didn't fancy being killed by some keyboard jockey with a fetish for remote murder. The blade made short work of the suits' controls, sparks flying as he jammed it home.

Then he slumped down on the nearest armour corpse as the adrenaline drained away. What he really wanted now was a good cuppa. Small chance of that here. He found a bottle of water on the floor, but it wasn't really the same.

10

Warden's eyes narrowed as he surveyed the carnage, a sure sign that he wanted to swear. Five Marines dead, three wounded so severely that they'd be little use for days or even weeks, several others carrying minor injuries. They had captured the solar farm and the ship, it was true, but the cost had been high.

His HUD flashed a clear signal. The overwatch team hadn't seen any more movement and were heading over in the rovers. He acknowledged it with a glance, confirming their update was read and understood.

Warden turned his attention to the damage that Marine X had caused with grenades and heavy gunfire. No hull ruptures, it seemed, but one end of the balcony had been destroyed, and twisted metal blocked the port door. Other than that, the damage appeared to be cosmetic and there was no reason to think the ship wasn't spaceworthy. He sent Patel to the other side to see if the blocked door still worked.

Then he turned to the elephant in the room, namely the pods that had surprised the boarding party. He walked over to one and peered through the glass cover. Inside, a winged alien floated in a thick, translucent gel. There were sixteen pods in total, all occupied.

Two held enormous hulking brutes like the one they had killed in the base.

He turned to Milton. "They're clones. The bloody aliens are using our own bloody cloning tech against us. They must have captured military files on the Ark ship; these are definitely mil-tech clones."

"Yes, sir. Not the same as ours, though. Look at all the scales and the strange eyes. Our geneticists don't do things like that; they keep even the mil-tech clones as close to human as possible. Wings notwithstanding, of course," said Milton.

Warden closes his eyes for a moment, taking deep breaths and contemplating their next steps. Then he snapped back, alert and confident.

"Right, I want the casualties off the ship, and the rovers stowed somewhere safe. If we make it back, we'll land here and drive back to Ashton. Make sure the drivers have weapons, plenty of munitions and that they stay out of sight until we return. Get the techs working on the ship. If they can't get it flying, everything else we do here is a waste of time."

"Roger that," Milton replied.

"Marine X, get your arse down here," he bellowed. "Sergeant Milton, take a team through the ship again and make sure every single compartment is double checked. I don't want to be surprised by these things," he said, pointing at a pod that contained an alien clone that appeared to be the pilot or officer class.

"Then a weapons check. Reload magazines, search the ship for anything we can add to our armoury," he said, turning to Ten who had dropped down from the balcony.

"Prep for low-pressure boarding. Take half a squad and ransack the stores. Find any breathing apparatus or environment suits and bring them here," he turned again as Ten peeled off, "someone get this ramp down, and the rest of you, bring the arsenal aboard." He paused to look at his team then he clapped his hands. "Hop to it, people."

He paced around the room, looking at the controls and checking the systems. It was pretty familiar stuff but it seemed strange, outdated even.

Tech from an ancient Ark, he thought, centuries old.

He flipped up a cover and pressed the button it concealed. Warning beeps sounded, and lights appeared on the floors of the loading bays. Launch chairs rose from the floor space on both sides of the cloning bay. There were enough for more troops than would be deployed in one round of cloning. It made it easy to retrieve any planetside troops, even if more than one round of clones had been decanted during a mission.

Warden looked around as everyone got on with their assigned tasks. He assumed the dropship would navigate itself to the alien vessel and land in an enclosed bay. Low-pressure boardings were dangerous but he hoped it wouldn't be necessary.

Even if they didn't need to breach the outer hull of the ship, there was still a question over the alien's air. Just because they could breathe the air on New Bristol didn't mean the Marines would be able to breathe on the ship. Any difference in the gas mixture could cause problems, so he wanted to be sure that everyone had a reliable air supply for their breathing masks.

And he needed an option of last resort. That the aliens had clones altered everything. Every soldier they'd killed on New Bristol would be backed up, probably to the vessel in orbit. How long till they were decanted into new bodies and dropped back to the surface? Even if they didn't have cloning bays as part of the vessel, they might have more dropships. How many, he wondered, and how fast would they move?

He scratched his head and sighed as he walked into the cockpit. If his tech specialists couldn't get this thing in the air, they would need a new plan, fast.

Richardson looked up as he entered the cockpit. "Good news, sir. The ship's systems are intact. The aliens have things arranged just like we do in our own ships. Good job they stole our technology, I suppose. It looks like they haven't really changed everything. I reckon if we pulled the panels off, some of the circuits would be exactly as they were when they were designed."

"Great. Can you pilot it without knowing their language?"

"Don't need to, sir. Just need to identify the auto-pilot. The dropship will get us back to their ship on its own. I think we can work out the necessary basics in maybe ten more minutes? Just don't ask us to get into a dogfight, not that I imagine this crate has any weaponry to speak of. If they haven't changed basic cockpit layout, they probably won't have changed that either."

"Is there any way to tell how many dropships they have on their ship?" asked Warden hopefully.

"Not really, sir. If we spoke their language we could probably bring up an inventory, but that's about it," Richardson said apologetically.

"It'll be at least three," murmured Barlow. He cautiously pressed a button, then quickly pressed it again when the lighting panel above his head went out.

Warden and Richardson looked at him. He didn't seem to notice their stares. Warden coughed. "Would you care to explain, Corporal?"

Barlow looked up. "Hmm? Oh well, it's elementary really. This ship is the Something in Alien Three. So there must be at least two more dropships aboard the vessel unless they have really odd naming schemes."

"How do you know it's three?" asked Warden.

"It's written on the side of the ship. Also, on this panel here," Barlow said, pointing to a plaque with a series of symbols on the overhead bank of panels in front of the pilot's chairs.

"Yes, okay," said Warden slowly, as he contemplated the squiggles and dots which could have been an ancient Earth language for all the good it did him, "but how do you know that says that this is ship number three?"

"This bit," said Barlow pointing, "is the same as the bit on the third pod from the left on the fore and aft side of the clone bay. So my conclusion is it's their glyph for 'three'. Look, it's here on this button too," he said pointing to a button on the console, "so these buttons are probably two and four."

Warden looked as directed. Barlow had a gift for noticing these things and Warden couldn't fault his logic.

"I see. So at the very least they have two more dropships, which means at least thirty-two clones available to them, plus whatever crew or active troops are left on the mothership. If they have four dropships for a nice even number, they have forty-eight clones, ready to be deployed," said Warden. He slumped a little in his chair, thinking.

"How long would it take to decant an alien clone?"

Both techs shrugged. "No idea, sir. Probably about the same as ours, although they don't have to inject brain patterns via wormhole here. Corporal Wilson might know more."

"Right," said Warden, standing up decisively, "get this thing ready to fly as quickly as possible. If there's even a slim chance we can dock with the ship in orbit and complete the assault before they decant more clones, we need to take it. Every minute we waste here could make our task up there much more difficult."

"Yes, sir. One working dropship, coming right up."

11

Warden gritted his teeth as the acceleration of the dropship pushed him into the seat. The flight had started easily, like an ordinary aeroplane, but the ship had climbed quickly before standing on its tail to point straight up. And then the main engines had fired, rocketing the vessel towards escape velocity.

It took only twenty seconds or so to leave behind the atmosphere of the planet and reach the edge of space, but the g-force was extraordinary and, to Warden, it felt like it went on for hours.

Then it was over and, just like that, they were free of the planet's grip and on their way to orbit. The transition from the daylight of the atmosphere to the night-time environment of planetary orbit was stark and sudden, like turning off a light.

Warden had clipped his HUD to his belt for the launch. Richardson's jury-rigged countdown played through the ship's speakers so the Marines would know when main acceleration was coming and when they'd get the relief of it ending. Ten minutes was a good rule of thumb for this type of flight.

It was a desperate mission. Even at full strength, the risks would have been high. With A Troop depleted, no Command team and large parts of Section 3 currently dead, the attack was truly a forlorn hope. What they really needed was time. And B Troop, thought Warden, denied action by the destruction of the second cloning bay, to say nothing of C Troop, who were safely at home enjoying the luck of the draw.

Warden grinned grimly. C Troop would be doing more than the normal amount of cleanup and physical training at the moment. They'd 'won' the deployment lottery and been left back at base, but they would be working just as hard as A Troop, albeit with less risk of a gruesome death under an alien sky.

The pre-launch briefing had been short and the questions few. Now they flew in silence, HUDs off, weapons locked down, everyone focusing on what was to come.

Why were HUDs off for launch? Warden couldn't remember, but maybe it was something to do with safety. Black eyes, maybe? He shook his head; it didn't matter, the standing order was to launch with HUDs stowed.

In free fall, though, HUDs were safe, and Warden slipped his back on. The command panel he would have had on an RMSC drop-ship was absent, so he patched through to the pilot's view.

There was a moment of disorientation as he tried to work out what he was seeing. Then the grey, almost featureless, slab of the ship in front of them slid open to expose a docking bay.

"It's big," muttered Warden, surprised despite his long-nurtured cynicism, "very big." Around him, he could see that the Marines were similarly awed, all watching the pilot's feed.

"How does it look?" Warden asked.

"Coming on nice, sir," said Richardson. "Thrusters firing, nothing to do up here but watch. Very dull."

"Good, let's hope it stays that way."

In the last five decades, there had never been a need to breach an enemy ship, certainly not while under fire. The Marines were trained for it, of course, but they didn't have the kit. Their only option was to dock and if the alien ship took action against them, their assault would be over before it had properly started.

Warden looked around at the Marines of A Troop.

"Thirty seconds," said Richardson. "Matching velocities."

The thrusters fired again, more violently this time as the ship moved in towards its hanger.

"Weapons ready," ordered Warden as they passed into the shadow of the great ship and the thrusters fired again, slowing them still further. There was a ripple of movement amongst the Marines as they checked their weapons and kit one last time.

Then the view changed as they passed into the hanger. A clang reverberated through the hull, and everyone jumped.

"Docking complete," reported Richardson, "outer door closed, atmosphere coming in." And gravity, which returned with a welcome thump when the ship stopped moving, pushing everyone firmly into their seats.

Warden sent a command via the HUD for everyone to don their breathers until they could check the atmosphere against human tolerances. Pre-launch, he and Milton had made sure everyone understood to keep their breathers on until they were out of the hangar, as that would be the most easily vented compartment should any of the crew realise what was going on.

"Almost there," said Richardson, voice tense. "Ten seconds till doors open."

The commandos unstrapped and stood, checking weapons and lining up on the exit ramps.

"Doors open in three, two, one," said Richardson, punching the door control.

The Marines pounded down the ramps and sprinted for the exits, gathering in teams around each doorway. With the access cards retrieved from the dropship troops, they opened three doors simultaneously. Marine X and Warden's best-trained stealth troops slipped through the doors and moved into the giant ship to begin clearing the area.

Micro-drones followed, tracking each team so the rest of the Marines could follow closely behind without giving away their presence. Richardson stayed in the dropship, locking herself in and prepping for launch in case they had to evacuate early, although nobody really expected that to be a survivable experience.

Warden looked around before he left the room, found a storage locker that Richardson could see from the cockpit and dumped a bag in it. He saw Richardson hold up a small object in her hand and nod at him through the cockpit window. Warden nodded to her. If it all went to hell, Richardson had orders to launch the dropship and press the detonator before returning planetside.

Warden went through the door, following Marine X's team and waiting for something to give them away and sound the alarm.

12

Marine X had killed two aliens so far, taking them down before they knew he was there. Now he moved, unseen and silent, checking for movement as his team tidied up behind him and checked the rooms he'd skipped.

At the end of the corridor, his way was blocked by a bulkhead door. A quick glance through the porthole revealed an engineering bay. No sign of movement.

He opened the door and stepped inside. The room was long and closed off at the other end; this was the only entrance he could see. There was nobody around. He paced down the room slowly. He was on the port side of the vessel and heavy equipment was stacked against the exterior bulkhead. Guns, he decided; these were gun emplacements, and this was the servicing bay.

The huge room was open, but there were bulkheads between each gun that could be sealed if there was a breach. Damaged cannons could be easily accessed for repair or isolation and containment. There wasn't likely to be anyone in here, so he picked up his pace and jogged to the other end of the bay. Better to move quickly than risk getting sealed behind bulkheads and exposed to vacuum.

But the room was clear and he walked back down the bay,

reloading his weapon and updating the map for the rest of the troop as he went.

So far, the ship was symmetrical, which was hardly surprising. Most starships' layouts were designed to be easily understood, even in pitch blackness. Areas were repeated and identical apart from markings to show where you were in the ship. The weapons bay had glyphs near the doors and on each cannon, and though he couldn't read them, he knew they would tell the crew exactly where they were on the ship. He marked the room clear, glanced to the right where his team were catching up, then moved to the next door.

There was a thick transparent panel in the upper half of the door, and he tilted his head forward to glance through it. A barracks room with rows of sleeping compartments against the walls and in the middle of the room, four high, stretching from floor to ceiling.

Each bay was sealed with an opaque shutter. If the artificial gravity failed, which wasn't unlikely in an emergency, waking up to find that you were falling towards the middle of the room was not helpful. Better to be safely sealed in your sleeping pod. But that meant he couldn't see whether the compartments were occupied.

He paused for a few seconds, peering along the corridor between the pods, but no enemy personnel were visible.

Ten motioned for his team to join him and opened the door, sliding inside to check the first compartment. The translucent panel opened at his touch and revealed an empty bed. He checked two more compartments, both empty, before his team arrived and began clearing the other side of the room.

The fourth compartment was occupied, and Ten swiftly folded the pillow towards the head, jammed the barrel of his pistol into it and fired. There was a wet crunching sound, but the foam further muffled the noise of his already suppressed pistol. In a chamber like this, even a quiet weapon was loud enough to wake the enemy.

He heard a couple of dull shots behind him as the team dealt with more of the enemy. Another compartment, another swift execution, but their luck wouldn't hold much longer.

In the next compartment, the occupant was already moving as

Ten reached for the pillow. He cursed under his breath as the intended victim turned its head towards him and the eyes flicked open, widening in panic.

Ten fired but the alien was already moving. It shifted quickly, trying to sit up and twist out of the sleeping chamber. The shot went wide, thudding into the mattress. Then the alien slapped its left arm towards him, knocking the gun from Ten's hand. The alien began to shout, loudly. Ten yanked the arm, pulling the alien close then wrapping his right arm around its neck. He tightened the hold and fell back on the floor with the alien on top of him as it kicked and struggled.

He wrapped his legs around the alien's waist to control it and scrabbled for a knife, stabbing it into the alien's torso while trying to keep it quiet. It took too long, far too long. The alien kicked, struggled and gurgled as it died, but Ten could already hear other compartments opening around the room.

"Don't let them raise the alarm!" he called out as he flung the corpse away and rolled to his feet.

Ten snatched up his pistol and hurried to the open compartments, firing on instinct and without caution, trying to kill as many of the enemy as he could. He could hear the faint coughs of pistol fire around him from the rest of the team and, for a few glorious seconds, he thought they might recover the situation and stop it from becoming an absolute shit show.

Then someone found a rifle and he wasn't friendly.

Automatic weapons fire screamed through the barracks, rounds ricocheting from the sleeping compartments.

"Fuck!" shouted one of the Marines, Ten couldn't tell who, as they all sought cover.

Ten holstered his pistol and sheathed his knife, unslinging the alien rifle he carried across his back. His team were doing the same as they knelt or lay behind cover. Fortunately, the sleeping chambers were pretty solid, designed to protect an occupant from decompression, and they made good cover.

<Lieutenant, we're in the barracks, and it's gone hot. No alarm yet but it won't be long> he sent via his HUD.

<Understood> replied Warden. He sent a message to the entire team.

<Heads up! Switch to primary weapons, press hard and fast, expect resistance. Let's not give these bastards time to work out what's going on or where we are>

The map showed that they had swept about an eighth of the ship so far, including two dropship bays.

<Let's clear the barracks, secure the next bays, then find the bridge. No quarter to be given> ordered Warden.

Ten grinned, reached into a pouch, pulled out a grenade and threw it to the far end of the room.

"Flashbang," he shouted for the benefit of his team, then, "grenade," as he threw the second object. It wasn't exactly sporting to disorient the enemy and then throw a fragmentation grenade but the time for fair play was long gone.

He rolled over and up into a crouch behind the compartment that was his shelter, clapping his hands over his ears and squeezing his eyes shut. The HUDs lenses would block most of the flash and he had time and cover to his advantage.

After the second explosion, Ten hefted his weapon and advanced, quickly but quietly. He knew from experience that ear-splitting sounds could still be heard by the victims of a flashbang. Well, by humans, at any rate; he had no idea how the aliens might react. Fast and quiet, then. No shouting or screaming war cries, which was about the stupidest thing you could do in a situation like this.

Instead, he moved up the room like a panther searching for prey, rapidly but smoothly and on the balls of his feet. One round to the head or a couple to the chest of any alien he thought might still be able to move, then immediately on to the next. His HUD showed the bulk of A Troop already at the door of this barracks or the one on the other side of the ship. His job wasn't to be one hundred per cent sure about each enemy but to kill, injure or incapacitate so the Marines following could tidy up behind him.

There was a burst of fire from somewhere ahead but it wasn't aimed at him, and he sprinted around the side of a row of sleeping bays to find one determined alien, in its underwear, desperately trying to reload its rifle.

Ten coughed politely and, as it turned towards him, put a quick burst into its face.

"Sorry, old chum, good effort, though." A quick death was the best he could do.

There was a moment of sudden silence after the appalling noise of the grenades. No enemy movement, no shouts or shots. Ten looked around to double check then grabbed the alien's weapon, slamming a new magazine into it before reloading his other weapons.

<Lieutenant> sent Ten.

<Marine X. How's it going?>

<We're secure for the moment, but I'd be amazed if we didn't have a tough fight ahead> replied Ten. Then he turned to speak to his team. "There's a spare rifle here if anyone needs one."

Warden checked his HUD; the second barracks was secure. Two Marines were down, though – Maxwell and McDonald. Just twenty-five commandos left to finish the mission.

Will it be enough? he wondered.

13

"Barlow, Cooke, Goodwin! Get the drones out, full offensive mode. I want to know what's ahead and I want to know now," Warden called out. Milton had her half of the Troop lined up in the barracks opposite, ready to storm the next area of the ship. There were only two exits from each barracks, the ones they had entered by at port and starboard and one facing the front of the ship. Warden had sent Goodwin back out into the corridor, to the crossroads that ran between the two barracks, along with Lance Corporal Jean Bailey and her spotter, Marine Adam Parker.

The micro-drones went first, the smallest the tech-specialists had with them. Warden cursed their lack of equipment; a more established colony would have had far more toys for them to play with.

It was the specialist pico-drones he really missed, the ones normally used for exploring and mapping enemy buildings or vessels. They were tiny, fast and hard to detect, far smaller than the micro-drones which were a multi-purpose compromise.

In the sterile environment of a ship, especially one as densely fitted-out as this one appeared to be, the micro-drone wasn't nearly as discreet as he'd have liked. But it was still better than sticking your head around a corner and finding an enemy with a shotgun waiting for you.

The drones quickly added the next corridors, which were empty, to the floor plan. They couldn't get through bulkheads or locked doors but they were perfect for scouting open areas. Barlow sent an update identifying two doors at port and starboard as matches to the ones in the other docking bays.

It looked like they had found their objective. Between the remains of A Troop and those all-important dropship bays, there was a series of smaller rooms, possibly officer's quarters judging by the number of doors and size.

"Marines X, Fletcher and Harrington. Clear those rooms, quick as you can please. Techs, I want combat drones guarding those launch bay doors. Once we breach, attack the storerooms and armoury between the bays. Milton, once the cabins are clear, take the rest of your team through that dropship bay as fast as possible. Everyone else, keep your breathers handy in case of a hull breach," Warden ordered.

Ten was done with the first cabin before Warden had finished his orders and they swept from port to starboard along the corridor. Resistance was light, only a few rounds were discharged, and no fire-fight broke out. It was over in less than two minutes and Warden ordered an immediate assault on the bays.

The commandos surged forward, rushing for their assigned doors, the techs and sniper teams bringing up the rear. Warden's team stormed into the port dropship bay. Aside from markings and the dropship being clean of mud and dust, it was identical to the starboard bay. No enemies were visible, so they jogged across the hangar.

<Contact> Milton sent. Warden took cover and checked her view-point. They were taking fire from the other side of the hangar.

"Marine X, get that door open now, we need to flank them, Milton's team is under heavy fire in the other dropship bay."

Ten nodded grimly and sprinted to the door across the bay in the direction of the bow.

Warden issued orders rapidly, sending half his group through the door with Ten and the other half east into the armoury and workshop area that linked the two dropship bays. He sent the techs and the sniper teams toward the storage rooms. If the layout was symmetrical, when they reached the middle of the three storerooms, they could go north into the armoury and workshop area.

If the enemy were in there as well as the starboard dropship hangar, they would be caught between Warden's team on their port side, the techs and sniper teams coming from the aft and Marine X's group from the bow. They'd flip the enemy ambush on its head and turn the hunters into the hunted.

He checked Milton's view again. It was bad. Not everyone had found cover and casualties were mounting.

Warden sprinted starboard, cursing the doors that responded only slowly to his key card.

Too slow, too slow, he thought.

<We're on our way, Milton. Keep your heads down> he sent.

<It's a bit unfriendly in here, sir. Hope you can lighten the mood soon> she replied.

He reached the middle room, bursting in behind the techs as they reached the bow door.

"Go, go, go!" he yelled as he crossed the room, pressing his card against the lock. His HUD was alive with contact markers.

Ten and his team were in a firefight in the corridor.

Milton was still pinned down. The munition and repair equipment storage areas were well-defended.

Someone went down as Warden reached the last storeroom door. Behind it, the remnants of Milton's team were pinned in the hanger.

Warden crouched as it opened, bringing his carbine to his shoulder and wishing he had grabbed one of the more substantial alien weapons. No time for regrets, though. He leaned just far enough to his right to sight the weapon towards the wall opposite Milton, where the enemy was taking cover. They were on the balcony at the same height as him and on the floor below, all well sheltered from the Marines' fire. Lots of metal storage crates were clamped to the floor and the railings had safety panels to fill the gaps.

With a trio of whumpfs that sounded a lot like a fast-moving drift of snow falling off a roof, Warden launched a series of grenades at the balcony. He gave a count of one and then sighted roughly where the enemy was on the ground floor and pulled the trigger, keeping it depressed and controlling the muzzle climb as best he could while he emptied the magazine.

He ducked back into cover as he smoothly swapped the magazine, cycling through the views of his team, trying to get a better sight line of the area he'd hit. Nothing clear.

"Get me a drone in the hangar for fuck's sake! I don't care if it gets hit, we're losing people," he ordered. "We need visibility."

He leaned around the doorway again and emptied another magazine. He sprayed indiscriminately into the cloud of smoke and dust from the grenades, then took cover again. He wasn't likely to inflict any damage, but it should keep the enemy's heads down.

Finally, a drone made it into the hangar, hugging the ceiling as it scanned the huge bay. Ghostly red imagery overlaid his own view and now Warden knew where the enemy were. There was movement in the cloud, so at least one enemy was still active. He reloaded his carbine with grenades and a fresh magazine, slung it across his back and pulled out his pistol, suppressor already attached.

He threw two more grenades and sent a silent message to Milton's team.

<Flashbangs>

Then he ran through the doorway and along the balcony, directly at the aliens and into the smoke. He skidded to his knees as the first infra-red blob loomed out of the smoke before him. The greyness shifted and the kneeling alien seemed to coalesce out of the fog. It turned towards him, a look of horror on its face, as Warden's suppressor touched its forehead.

The weapon bucked and the alien fell back. Warden was already rising, rebreather on, moving into the smoke. It was risky, but the drone would have painted him a friendly blue and they didn't have the numbers to be cautious.

He took the next alien with three hurried rounds to the chest, not even stopping as he rounded the corner of the balcony and began to move down it. Another blob appeared, coughing in the swirling smoke, and Warden lifted his weapon. He heard the tell-tale pings of rounds bouncing off powered armour as the towering figure became visible. His heart pounded. It was one of the enormous brutes he had tackled planetside, only this time in full power armour.

Warden glanced despondently at his pistol. The alien hadn't seen him yet, but the smoke was clearing. He holstered his weapon and began to reach for another, staying as still as possible in the hope it wouldn't spot him.

Then the head snapped towards him, the helmet expressionless. Warden could almost see the alien's face, hear its grunt of surprise. He imagined the alien was looking at him and mouthing the equivalent of "What the fuck?"

Warden grinned lopsidedly and threw his weapons to the floor at the feet of the gigantic trooper. It looked down for a moment then looked back up as Warden waved and bravely ran away. He took three steps, unslinging his carbine as he ran towards the corner, then dove for cover through an open door.

The explosion of the grenades he'd gifted the alien was deafening. His ears rang and the air was acrid with smoke. He checked his HUD and realised where he was. Lifting his head from the deck, he saw two alien troopers gaping at him. He was in the armoury. Behind the enemy. Not the ideal place to take cover.

Their weapons came around and he had nowhere to go. His teams were behind cover but the space between them and Warden was wide open. He rolled and alien rounds chattered from the barrels. He kept rolling, waiting for the impact. Then he hit a wall and fumbled at his carbine, scrabbling to point it at the enemy.

He blinked. Both alien troopers were dead.

Ten stood over them, one foot on the crushed neck of an alien. Something dripped in his left hand and in his right was the large, glowing alien knife.

"I fucking love this knife, Lieutenant," said Ten with obvious glee.

Warden looked at the body and back at the head Ten gripped by its hair. He'd taken it clean off with the knife. Then he casually tossed it out through the door, towards the spot in the hangar where the aliens had been. There were several bursts of fire.

"For fuck's sake! Was that Ten? Would you tell him to stop doing that, Lieutenant, it's not bloody funny anymore," Milton shouted into her radio.

Warden sucked in a lungful of air and rolled onto his back laughing, "Sorry, Sergeant, not this time."

14

"What's the casualty list, Milton?"

"We lost Barber, Mitchell and Lee, sir, and Corporal Campbell is mortally injured. Some further injuries but nothing serious. All told, we have twenty-one personnel," she replied.

Warden clenched his fist, the nails digging into his palm. The odds were not in their favour. They still had a substantial portion of the ship to clear and no way of knowing how many enemy combatants were still active. There could be half a dozen ship crew or thirty power-armoured troopers waiting for them.

"Wilson, what's our drone situation?" he asked, turning to the corporal who was the most senior of their tech specialists.

"We lost a few in that engagement, sir. We have a handful of micro-drones but only two functioning combat drones. Not that they're much use on board this ship," he said apologetically.

"We need visibility, Wilson. I want any drones you have out there mapping the rest of the ship and gathering intel. If the combat drones can take any action, do so. We don't need to worry about discretion now," said Warden.

"Can do, sir, but it won't leave us any spares. When we're planetside, we won't have surveillance until we can fabricate more drones.

And the colonists lost their satellite network, as well as a lot of their communications grid. Do you want us to go ahead, bearing that in mind?"

Warden considered for a moment, then nodded. "We don't have a choice, Corporal. If we don't complete our mission here, we won't be getting planetside anyway. Even if we retreated, they have three more dropships, and we'd be facing overwhelming odds within twenty-four hours if they deployed just the clones they already have. I'd rather have this ship crippled and be blind planetside than face those odds. Be careful with the combat drones but don't hesitate to sacrifice them if you can take out an armoured trooper or we get another firefight like this one, okay?"

"Yes, sir. Thank you, sir," Wilson nodded and turned to his colleagues. They set up out of the way and launched all their drones, the tiny hummingbirds zipping off to map the next area of corridors. The two combat drones, much larger but with only light arms, launched last. They hovered, advancing more cautiously, following the plans left by their smaller brethren.

Warden surveyed the rest of his team, only twenty strong with Richardson in the dropship. He frowned.

"Moyes, is that a railgun on your back?"

"Yes, sir," the young Marine replied.

"Didn't I specifically order that we weren't to use railguns due to the risk of venting atmosphere?"

"I haven't used it, sir," she replied.

"I meant that we should leave them behind. Why did you bring it?"

"I thought if we had it, we could use it, sir. My sniping instructors always told me to be prepared."

"That's good advice, Moyes, but please tell me you understand why I don't want to expose us all to vacuum when we don't even have environment suits?"

She nodded. "Yes, sir, I just wanted to be able to vent the atmosphere if you needed me to. Like, if we shot some rounds through their bridge, the crew might find it hard to control the ship.

They don't seem to be well prepared for a boarding action. Maybe they won't have their breathers at hand?"

Warden blinked. He turned to look at Milton who was having obvious difficulty stifling the impulse to laugh. He turned back to Moyes then called Lance Corporal Bailey and Marine Findlay over.

"Moyes, tell Bailey and Findlay what you just suggested."

She looked a little shy about the prospect of suggesting her idea to the older Marines and Warden realised just how young she was. It was easy to lose track of such things when operating in clones, but his HUD confirmed Moyes was only twenty-two. She'd been in the Royal Marine Cadet program while pursuing her degree in fine art, of all things.

Moyes could easily have gone straight into the officer training course but instead had chosen the rapid acceleration track which would take her through the non-commissioned ranks before giving her the opportunity to attend officer training and be commissioned. It was an unusual route, but it spoke to a deep level of commitment and forethought.

Moyes cleared her throat and said, "Well, I thought that if we used the alien's railgun against the ship's bridge, we could vent their atmosphere into space. Even if they do have environment suits in there, it would be a bit inconvenient for them."

"Assessment, Bailey?" Warden asked.

"I can't think of a reason we shouldn't, sir. If we can reach the corridor outside the bridge, we would have to shoot through one wall and out the other side. That would give us decent penetration, and if we can shoot from a doorway we can retreat quickly, seal the door behind us, and we'll be secure. If they have power armour in there, though, you can bet they'll follow us."

"I can rig tripwires with our spare grenades," Ten suggested.

"That might work," said Bailey, nodding.

Warden walked over to the techs. "Report."

"We have a good visualisation of this section, sir," Wilson said, looking up. He pointed to a data slate and highlighted several rooms. "This is a cloning bay and, look, the monitors show clones being activated as we speak. No way of knowing how long that will take. This is a cafeteria," he said, pointing at a new spot, "and what looks like a recreation room, currently unoccupied. This is a medical bay, there's a couple of staff in it, presumably medics. We can't see inside the next three rooms so we'll need to open those bulkhead doors to get drones in but we have the general corridor layout, and there aren't any nasty surprises in the areas we can see. We have strong emissions from the other side of the bulkheads, so it's reasonable to assume we're not far from their communications and bridge areas, assuming they've got similar ship layouts and functionality to our own, which has been true so far."

"Marine X, get those rooms cleared, pronto. Everyone else, ready to move out. I want to breach those doors and then get the drones in immediately."

They moved out, going about their tasks efficiently. The techs gathered their gear and went mobile, ready to support if necessary and preparing their drones for the breach of the bulkhead doors. Warden pulled the snipers' spotters from that duty and assigned them to the breaching team. At this range, the snipers' only role was to use the railgun and they only had one, so the other two would look after Moyes.

<Cleared> came across the HUD from Marine X.

<Move> Warden broadcast. The commandos dashed forward, in position in under thirty seconds.

Marines stepped forward to each of the three sealed doors, spinning the wheel locks and pulling them wide open. The micro-drones zipped through, visually clearing the corridors beyond in seconds. Warden checked the feeds and issued the next order to move.

Ten led the way through the starboard door and stormed into a communications room, glowing knife in one hand and pistol in the other. The aliens inside weren't in a position to fight back; they barely freed their sidearms before Ten finished them.

Warden closed the feed from Ten and moved as the team cleared two staterooms on the port side of the ship. One large room between the communications room and the staterooms remained. He closed on it at the same time as Ten, and they burst through the door together.

It wasn't surprising to find a war room with a large illuminated data table showing a map of the solar system and images of New Bristol. There were displays on all the walls. The surprise came from the two alien troopers in powered-armour who were waiting inside.

Warden admitted to himself later that the shock had thrown off his response time. Not so for Penal Marine X. Ten threw himself forward at the nearest enemy, his pistol firing as he closed the gap.

Warden targeted the second figure and emptied his magazine. He knew the alien rifle was powerful, but he wasn't taking any chances with powered armour. It wouldn't be a waste of ammo if he took down this trooper.

Ten dropped his pistol and switched the knife to his right hand. He batted the alien trooper's weapon aside and closed into a close grapple. His left arm wrapped around the alien's right and the knife came down hard, punching in and out through the weaker points in the alien's armour. Under the armpit, the neck, the join between thigh and waist.

Warden's alien staggered back, knocked off its feet by the rounds striking its helmet and chest. The lieutenant sprang forward, pulling the twin to Ten's knife from its sheath and thumbing the mechanism as he landed on top of the trooper. He snarled as he raised the knife to finish his opponent and then let his hand drop. The front of the helmet was gone, smashed to pieces, and the face behind it was shattered. The rifle, it seemed, had been more than a match for the armour.

Warden got to his feet and sheathed the knife. He rammed a fresh magazine into the rifle and looked around.

"Charges, sir?"

"You think the next room is the bridge?"

"Only two doors and they're close together. Looks like one room to me, Lieutenant."

"Go ahead then. Let's finish this."

<Move up, Moyes> Warden ordered.

Warden pointed his rifle at the doors while Ten set the charges. The other teams took up positions in the doorways and corridors that had sight lines to the room they'd decided must be the bridge.

"How long, Marine X?" he asked.

"Want it good and efficient or quick and unreliable?"

"I'm an officer, Marine X. I want it done quickly and I want it done well."

"Bloody typical," Ten muttered, though hardly sotto voce.

"Do you want another thirty days on your sentence, Marine X?" Warden asked.

"Oh, yes please, sir? Can I? I do so love coming to shitholes and looking after moisture farmers and asteroid miners. Another couple of minutes should do it, if you want my best work."

"Cut the comedy routine, Ten. Just get it done."

"It'll never be enough, I tell you! As if I have anything else in my life."

Warden rolled his eyes and checked the HUD readouts again. He glanced down at Ten's work; he was almost done.

A metallic whir from his left drew his attention. The wheel lock on the bulkhead door was turning. Warden's eyes tracked down to the cluster of grenades and the jury-rigged mechanism Ten had attached to them and the door. It was already armed. His head snapped back to Ten, oblivious and muttering under his breath.

As the wheel creaked ominously, Warden shot out, stooping as he moved, his arms tucking under Ten's armpits and lifting him as he headed for the doorway. "What the..." was all that Ten managed to splutter before the grenades behind them detonated.

The blast slammed into Warden's back and punched him sideways into the room with Ten under him. He slammed into the door frame on his way through, hearing at least one rib break. *Bollocks,* he thought, *I don't have time for this.* Worse, he'd ended up lying on top of a prone Ten in an entirely unflattering position.

Automatic weapons fire erupted behind him as Warden staggered to his feet. Ten stood up too and glared at Moyes, who'd been dragged back out of the way by Bailey and was staring at him in shock.

"Not a word," he growled.

Warden clutched his side and gritted his teeth. Ten looked him up and down and swore. Then he pulled an auto-injector from a belt pouch and slammed it into Warden's thigh before the lieutenant could protest.

"Shut up, Lieutenant. I heard the rib break and you need to stay functional. Unless you want to stay behind when we blow this rust bucket," Ten said.

The drug flooded through Warden and the pain in his chest faded into the background.

"What does it look like?" he asked.

Ten grabbed a rifle and risked sticking his head out to check the corridor. His reward was a sustained burst of fully automatic weapon fire. The rounds were ricocheting around the whole corridor as Ten jerked back into the room.

"Bloody hellfire! It's one of those big bastards in heavy power armour. He's only got a massive Gatling gun on each arm."

<Lieutenant, we have people down> sent Milton, <we're pulling back; nothing is getting through that thing's armour>

<Understood, Milton, the grenades didn't faze it. The armour must be heavier than we've seen before>

Warden turned to Moyes. "Marine, want to show us what you can do with that?"

She gulped. "I don't have a clear shot, sir."

She was right; it would be suicide to stick her head into that corridor and try to aim at that thing.

Bailey solved it. She threw something into the corridor and pulled Warden further into the room, leaving nothing but the wall of the room between Moyes and the gargantuan alien.

"The reflection, Moyes, check it, fire and adjust. The rifle is semi-automatic. Don't think, just shoot."

Moyes looked through the doorway; the object was a display Bailey had grabbed off a desk. The surface wasn't mirrored, but it was reflective enough to give a distorted view of the corridor. She squinted to pick out details, matching them to the layout she had in her HUD, then she brought the rifle to bear.

The railgun spat and the sabot tore through the wall.

"To the left, Moyes," Ten called out.

She adjusted the angle and fired again.

"That's it!" Ten shouted gleefully. "Pile on."

Moyes fired again, adjusted a fraction to the left and fired a fourth time.

"Nice, throw it to me, Moyes," Ten shouted. She tossed the railgun to him, and he shouldered it, leaned out into the corridor and fired again. "Done," he said, handing the rifle back to her, "nicely done, newbie. You're empty, reload."

"How many magazines do you have?" asked Warden.

"Five, sir," Moyes replied.

Well, that really was prepared.

"How do you feel about filling that bridge room with as many as you can get out?" suggested Warden. Moyes nodded.

<Milton. Breathers on and pull everyone back through the bulkheads, we'll take it from here. Let me know when you're clear> Warden sent through the UD. He turned to Ten and Bailey.

"Covering fire for the retreat. Breathers on." He slipped his mask up and over his nose and mouth and flipped it on.

Ten and Bailey let loose a few bursts down the corridor before Milton confirmed everyone else was back through the bulkhead and it was sealed.

"Let rip, Moyes," said Warden.

Moyes moved to the doorway and fired five rounds, ejecting the magazine and emptying the next into the bridge room as well. At least one must have penetrated the outer hull as an awful whistling began to suck the atmosphere from the ship.

<That's it, everyone out> Warden ordered and they retreated as fast as they could. They slammed the door behind them and spun the wheel but already the oxygen level was well down. They still needed their breathers.

"Richardson, can we get any more of the dropships down? How much time would it take if we can?"

"Sir, we might be able to. We'd need a tech to operate them, though. A few minutes for each dropship, maybe."

"Great. Get going, folks, I want those dropships on the surface and under our control. Milton, I want overwatch on the dropship bays. Let's make this an orderly retreat and deal with any crew we've missed before they have a chance to hit back." They'd lost Fletcher and Parker when the monster on the bridge had attacked and he didn't want to lose anyone else on the retreat.

Warden got back to the dropship bay more or less intact. He could feel a dull ache from his ribs though and his back ached. If he pushed it, he would be out of action himself.

This had not been a good day, but at least it was almost over. *Nothing much left to do now but clean up*, he thought.

Then the flashing red lights and a klaxon started.

"What the hell is that? Anyone got an idea what's going on? Come on, people – is the bridge crew still alive?"

It was a long, agonising minute before Richardson responded.

"Err. Yeah, we have a bit of a problem, sir. We may not have as much time as we thought."

"Spit it out, Richardson."

"We're falling out of orbit. Either someone scuttled the ship or we damaged something important a bit prematurely, sir. Maybe six minutes before it's going to get a bit dicey launching these dropships. As soon as we hit the upper atmosphere, it'll get really bumpy and very hot very quickly."

"Acknowledged. Has anyone got another dropship ready yet? We're in this bay and I don't see a tech inside the cockpit." Six minutes wasn't long to get to the next bay.

"We've got two more going, sir. Can you get to the port bay? It's closer than the stern one?" Goodwin responded.

"Roger that," Warden responded, turning to his snipers and Marine X. "Get moving and keep your eyes peeled. If the ship was scuttled, we might not be alone."

They moved out, darting across the dropship bay and towards the storerooms, moving fast. Warden ignored the tightness in his chest, gritting his teeth at the grinding sensation.

<Four minutes, Lieutenant. You need to get a shift on> sent Milton.

<Don't worry about us> he responded as they passed through the second storeroom, <just make sure all the dropships are ready to go>

A chatter of fire from behind made him turn his head.

"Moyes, get the lieutenant out of here, now! I'll hold these bastards!" Ten shouted over his shoulder.

Moyes dropped the railgun and inserted herself under Warden's arm. They started to jog as fast as Warden could manage with her supporting him.

"Lieutenant, you're bleeding. There's blood all over my hand," she panted.

"Don't worry about it," he replied through gritted teeth as they reached the dropship hangar, "it's not my body anyway." Probably explained why a broken rib was giving him so much trouble though, and why he was suddenly feeling cold. He'd probably caught some shrapnel when the giant alien had triggered Ten's booby trap.

Then they were at the ramp of the dropship, pushing past Milton who was crouched at the base firing bursts across the bay. Warden tried to turn but Moyes insisted and bundled him up the ramp. She and Goodwin forced him into a chair and strapped him in.

"Get that stupid bastard Marine X back here on the double," he slurred. Something was making his forearm hurt; he looked down to see a needle sticking out of it and frowned. *Where had that come from?* he wondered.

He heard shouting in the background, gunfire; then the world swam in front of his eyes for a moment or two.

Warden felt his stomach lurch, the distinctive sensation of a dropship entering the atmosphere.

"Back with us, Lieutenant?" said Ten, grinning from the seat opposite. Warden blinked. He must have blacked out for a few minutes. He looked down to see a blood pack attached to his chest and a tube leading to the needle in his arm. Well, that was a bit worrying. Judging by how alert he felt, they'd given him a combat stimulant as well.

"What happened? Milton?"

She was sitting next to Ten.

"We got two of the dropships ready, but you came under attack as you retreated. You've been bleeding for a while now. We've slapped a bandage on it, but you'll need some attention once we hit the ground. The aliens backed off when most of you got to the ship and we laid down enough fire for Ten to reach us. We dropped the moment the ramp was sealed. Richardson hit the detonator as soon as we were clear. It blew a hole in the hangar and caused a fair bit of damage. I don't think they'll be able to pull the ship out of its decaying orbit but we're monitoring it."

"Good work, everyone. Good work," Warden said, tilting his head back as the world shook and went dark around him.

EPILOGUE

"Captain? Can you hear me, Captain Atticus?" asked Wilson, leaning over the open pod.

Atticus raised his eyelids, blinking against the harsh light of the EDB. His new eyes stung and he felt strange. It was always strange waking up in a new body. Even though the blank clones came in very few varieties, a new one always seemed unfamiliar. The muscles hadn't been used for ages. Neither had the brain, for that matter.

He reached up to feel his face, a habit that he'd had for years. The facial features were always the last part of the clone that the tank grew after the imprint was designated to a particular blank. Essentially, the face was finished last and often took a few extra hours to settle in. The old joke was that if you played with your face before it had settled, it would set in a strange shape.

The earliest blanks, when the cloning technology had first been deployed, had been left complete but the result was that an entire deployment of troops would look exactly the same, which caused an astonishing number of problems. Instead, a close approximation of the person's real face was built in the final stages of clone deployment. It added hours to the process but it was better in the long run.

Wilson gripped his wrist before he could reach his face. His fingers felt odd on his skin.

"Wait, sir. We have to tell you something."

Atticus croaked, "What?" His voice sounded strange.

The cloning specialist looked a bit uncomfortable.

"We haven't been able to get our cloning bays working yet, sir. We had to improvise to get you redeployed."

"What is it?" Atticus demanded, trying to get the hang of his vocal chords.

"Barlow, whatever it is can wait. I need to talk to the captain. Just hold your horses and I'll get to you in a minute," Warden said. He moved into Atticus's eye line, supporting himself awkwardly on a crutch. "Don't panic, Captain, but what Wilson is dancing around is that we had to redeploy you in an enemy clone. You're in a military body, sir, just not a human one."

Atticus pulled his wrist from Wilson's grip and raised his hand. It was humanoid. Opposable thumb and four fingers, albeit unusually long and delicate. The palms were soft but the back of the hand was covered in scales.

"Oh. Shit. I'm an alien," Atticus sighed. "You really had to put me in an enemy clone? Are things that desperate?"

"I don't know, sir," said Warden, "but we're still growing new clones in the remaining bay and repairing the civilian one. I thought we should at least try this, though, because we captured three alien dropships since you went down. We have dozens of their clones and a working bay in each of the dropships, so a trial seemed like a good idea, and I didn't think you'd be happy if I used anyone else. I'm concerned they might have more troops deployed across the planet already. We have no way of knowing how many dropships landed or when," Warden explained. "We destroyed the ship they had in orbit, but that doesn't mean we're done with them."

"So we're trapped planetside and the aliens could have a battalion of soldiers somewhere on New Bristol?" Atticus asked.

"No, sir, that's what I've been –" Barlow started from the corner of the room but Warden cut him off, "Marine, I will get to you in a minute."

Atticus put an arm on Warden's shoulder and pulled himself upright.

"No, let him speak, Warden. He looks like he might burst. What's so urgent, Barlow?"

"They're not aliens, Captain," the tech specialist said.

There was a chorus of disagreement around the room and Atticus waved his scaled hand for silence.

"How do you come to that conclusion, Barlow?" looking at his hand as if to emphasise the evidence to the contrary.

"I thought something seemed odd, so I've been examining the bodies and equipment. I sampled the DNA of a few of the clones and ran it through the colony's sequencer. It's human, or at least, mostly human."

"You mean these are human military clones? But they have a different language, different character sets to any Sol culture. They even have new technology like that chameleon coating. Are you saying they're from Sol? A black op perhaps from another government or a corporation?" Warden asked.

"Not sure where they came from, sir, but the bodies are human. Brains too. I don't think these are aliens in human clones. I think you'd have to clone an alien brain format to be able to imprint an alien mind on a blank," he said, turning to Wilson for support.

"That makes a lot of sense, sir," said Wilson, "I was surprised when we were able to deploy you to that blank. I thought they must have created an interface to edit their pattern so it would fit a human brain. We can't imprint a human on a gorilla brain; the structure isn't similar enough. If we meet an actual alien species, they'd need to adjust the brain of the blanks they were using at a minimum or else they'd never be able to imprint to them. The rest could stay human but they couldn't get away with it without changing that."

"Can you be more specific about who these people are, Barlow?" Atticus asked.

"Only if we contact Sol, sir. They might have records of the Lost

Arks and we could compare the DNA we have here with the blanks that went out with the arks that went missing in this region. The earliest ark ships didn't even carry blanks; they pre-dated cloning, so we can rule those out. We could rule out more recent ones if we knew when some parts of the DNA of our basic and military blanks were first used," Barlow confirmed. "I'd need to contact HQ and send them a lot of data, though."

"Noted. Draft a report and I'll speak to HQ, explain the situation. Do we still have wormhole communications?" Atticus said, turning to Warden.

"No, sir," said the Lieutenant, shaking his head, "they went down at some point while we were dealing with the alien, I mean, enemy base. I'm expecting it back up in a few hours, though. We prioritised it so we could get updates and in case we needed more deployments."

"Okay. Get to it then, Barlow, we still need something to send when we have communications back up."

"How are you feeling, sir?" Warden asked.

"I seem to have picked up a bit of a skin complaint," said Atticus, staring at the back of his hand, "but I'm definitely better than last time we spoke. I need to get up to date. What's our current strength?"

Warden gave a rapid account of everything that had happened since Atticus had died.

"So we're down to twenty, including you, Captain."

Atticus frowned.

"That could be better, but it could be a lot worse, Lieutenant. I'm sure our people sold themselves dearly."

"They did, sir. We captured three of the four enemy dropships as well as a good number of their clones, including some heavily modified for combat. We also have a lot of their armour, weapons and munitions. It's good gear, some of it is better than ours."

"Well done, Lieutenant. Give me a moment to put something on and then I need to see the governor."

"She's waiting outside for you, sir. I told her we were going to try to deploy you into an enemy clone."

Atticus nodded and began to get dressed. He slipped some underwear on without daring to look at what these people might use; he would worry about that later. At least this body wasn't permanent. As long they could still back up their imprints, he'd be able to get home and leave this body for fertiliser.

He'd worn plenty of military clones in the past, but this one was different. The vision was particularly sharp and his hearing was excellent. He rapped a knuckle against the scales on the back of his arm. Tough but flexible. Nice, but he still wanted to get out of this body as soon as he could. He sighed and opened the door, stepping into the room beyond.

"Governor Denmead. How is New Bristol holding up?" he said, wondering if his scales were showing the blushing sensation he could feel creeping up his neck.

"Captain Atticus, glad to see you back on your feet," said the governor, barely glancing at his new body, "or on someone's feet, at least. We're doing as well as can be expected, given the week we've had. Let's go outside, and you can see for yourself." She hadn't batted an eyelid when confronted with his strange new body. A governor of the old school; not easily fazed.

An elevator took them to the roof. The building stood only four storeys above the ground but Ashton was a new colony city and lacked the horrific concrete canyons common to the metropolises of Earth or Mars.

"You can see the damage," Denmead said, pointing at a number of locations across the city that had collapsed or were still smoking. "We've lost a lot of people too, and even if we had a cloning bay, it would take months to grow enough blanks to deploy everyone."

"Warden tells me the enemy had four dropships but only one at their planetside base. There could be more of them out there. If I were them, I'd have landed across the planet and set up more than one base, then gathered intelligence about the colony. I'm not sure their grasp of strategy is that good, though. They strike me as a touch brash. Satellites down, I assume? Drones up?"

Warden shook his head. "We don't have long-range scouting

drones, sir. We're repairing the fabricators and the production facilities and arming the citizens with whatever we can scrape together."

Atticus thought about this for a moment as he stared across the smoking city. Then he nodded.

"We need to reassess our priorities; arming civilians won't help if we have hundreds of enemy troops out there. Let's get inside and take a hard look at the numbers," Atticus said.

They took a final look across the city and then turned to leave the roof. There was a beep from a communicator in Governor Denmead's jacket pocket. She took it out and flipped it open. "Yes, Johnson. What is it?"

"Governor, we need you in the command centre urgently."

"We were just on our way. What's wrong, Johnson? Don't be coy, spit it out, man!" she said, a hint of impatience in her tone.

"A beacon, ma'am, on the edge of the system. Ships are dropping out of hyperspace," he said, his voice betraying a definite hint of panic. Denmead made a mental note to speak to him about the importance of remaining calm for the citizens of New Bristol.

"It's just the fleet, Johnson. We requested support when we called in the Marines," she said, turning to Atticus and rolling her eyes apologetically. Atticus frowned, the expression amplified by his inhuman face, and glanced at Warden, who was looking distinctly worried. *What's wrong with them?* Denmead wondered.

"But there are no transponder signals, Governor," said Johnson, now sounding truly scared. "It's not our fleet. I think it's them, ma'am. I think it's the aliens."

Denmead took a couple of seconds to digest this.

"We're on our way, Johnson."

She turned to Atticus and Warden and gave them a brittle smile.

"Well, it could be worse. It could be raining."

THANK YOU FOR READING

Thank you for reading Commando, Book One in the Royal Marine Space Commando series. We hope you enjoyed the book and that you're looking forward to reading the next two entries in the series, Guerrilla and Ascendant, which are out now. We're writing the fourth book, Gunboat, now and books five and six are fully outlined.

It would help us immensely if you would leave a review on Amazon or Goodreads, or even tell a friend you think would enjoy the series, about the books.

In Guerrilla, you'll find out more about the Marines as well as the invaders of New Bristol and where they came from. Lieutenant Warden will have to lead his Marines into the heart of enemy territory and bring the war to them. Meanwhile, Captain Atticus, Governor Denmead and the civilian militia of New Bristol will have to protect the colony from the invasion.

Guerrilla is out now and you can read the prologue in the next pages.

SUBSCRIBE AND GET A FREE BOOK

Want to know when the next book is coming and what it's called?

Would you like to hear about how we write the books?

Maybe you'd like the free book, Ten Tales: Journey to the West?

You can get all this and more at imaginarybrother.com/journeytothewest where you can sign up to the newsletter for our publishing company, Imaginary Brother.

When you join, we'll send you a free copy of Journey to the West, direct to your inbox*.

There will be more short stories about Ten and his many and varied adventures, including more exclusive ones, just for our newsletter readers as a thank you for their support.

Happy reading,
Jon Evans & James Evans

We hope you'll stay on our mailing list but if you choose not to, you can follow us on Facebook or visit our website instead.

imaginarybrother.com

* We use Bookfunnel to send out our free books. It's painless but if you need help, they'll guide you through so you can get reading.

facebook.com/ImaginaryBrotherPublishing

ALSO BY JAMES EVANS AND JON EVANS

Also by James Evans

James is writing the Vensille Saga, an epic fantasy tale that begins with A Gathering of Fools and continues with A Gathering of Princes. The third book, A Gathering of Arms will be out in 2019.

A Gathering of Fools

Marrinek has fought his last war.

Once an officer in the Imperial Army, he has been betrayed, captured and named traitor. His future now holds only imprisonment and death - but that doesn't stop him dreaming of revenge.

Krant lives a clerk's life of paperwork and boredom until a chance meeting with an Imperial courier rips his world apart and sets him on a new course. Sent abroad with only the mysterious Gavelis for company, Krant faces an impossible task with no hope of success.

For two years, Adrava has hidden from her husband's enemies. But her refuge is no longer safe and she must venture forth to seek justice at the end of a blade.

In Vensille they gather, fools seeking shelter from a storm that threatens to drown the city in blood and fire.

Also by Jon Evans

Jon is concentrating on the Royal Marine Commando series for the time being but is also writing a fantasy series. The Edrin Loft Mysteries follow the adventures of Edrin Loft, Watch Captain of the Thieftakers Watch House.

You can read the first book Thieftaker now.

Thieftaker

Why was the murder of a local merchant so vicious?

Mere days after he takes charge of the Old Gate Watch House, Captain Edrin Loft must solve a crime so shocking that even veteran Sergeant Aliria Gurnt finds it stomach turning. With no witnesses or apparent motive for the crime, finding the culprit seems an impossible task.

But Loft has new scientific methods to apply to crime fighting. His first successful investigation caused a political scandal that embarrassed the Watch. Promotion to his own command was the solution. Known as The Thieftakers, they are the dregs of the Kalider City Watch, destined to spend the rest of their careers hunting criminals in the worst neighbourhoods. After all, what fuss could he cause running down thieves and murderers in the slums?

Old Gate and this murder might be the perfect combination of place and crime to test his theories. The Thieftakers are the best Kalider has at tracking criminals, and Loft must teach them the investigative skills to match.

Can he validate his theories and turn the Thieftakers into the first detectives in Kalider?

ABOUT THE AUTHORS JAMES EVANS

James has published the first two books of his Vensille Saga and is working on the third, as well as a number of other projects. At the same time, he is working on follow-up books in the RMSC series with his brother Jon.

You can join James's mailing list to keep track of the upcoming releases, visit his website or follow him on social media.

jamesevansbooks.co.uk

facebook.com/JamesEvansBooks

twitter.com/JamesEvansBooks

amazon.com/author/james-evans

goodreads.com/james-evans

bookbub.com/authors/jamesevans3

ABOUT THE AUTHORS JON EVANS

Jon is a new sci-fi author & fantasy author, whose first book, Thief-taker is awaiting its sequel. He lives and works in Cardiff. He has some other projects waiting in the wings, once the RMSC series takes shape.

You can follow Jon's Facebook page where you'll be able to find out more about the first trilogy of the RMSC series and the upcoming sequel, Gunboat.

If you join the mailing list on the website, you'll get updates about how the new books are coming as well as information about new releases and the odd insight into the life of an author.

jonevansbooks.com

facebook.com/jonevansauthor

amazon.com/author/jonevansbooks

goodreads.com/jonevans

bookbub.com/authors/jon-evans

instagram.com/jonevansauthor

Printed in Great Britain
by Amazon